C000173861

Pleasure Bound

Also in the *X Libris* series:

Pleasure Bound

Susan Swann

LIBRIS

An *X Libris* Book

First published by X Libris in 1997

Collection copyright © Susan Swann 1997

'Domia' first appeared in *Decadence* magazine,
copyright © Susan Swann 1994

The moral right of the author has been asserted.

*All characters in this publication are
fictitious and any resemblance to real
persons, living or dead, is purely coincidental.*

All rights reserved.
No part of this publication may be reproduced,
stored in a retrieval system, or transmitted, in
any form or by any means, without the prior permission
in writing of the publisher, nor be otherwise circulated
in any form of binding or cover other than that in which
it is published and without a similar condition including
this condition being imposed on the subsequent purchaser.

A CIP catalogue record for this book
is available from the British Library.

ISBN 0 7515 1872 7

Photoset in North Wales by
Derek Doyle & Associates, Mold, Clwyd
Printed and bound in Great Britain by
Clays Ltd, St Ives plc

X Libris
A Division of
Little, Brown and Company (UK)
Brettenham House
Lancaster Place
London WC2E 7EN

Contents

Pleasure Bound

The Seven-Year Itch

STACEY PLUMPED UP the pillows and leaned against the headboard. She could hear Ross moving around downstairs and guessed that he was preparing a special breakfast tray.

She sighed. He tried, poor darling. But whatever he did she knew it would make no difference. They were in a rut. She still loved him, but the spark had gone. They were . . . *comfortable* together. Cosy. Still, what could you expect after seven years of marriage?

When the door opened and Ross came in, she pasted a smile on her face. After all, you were supposed to be happy on your birthday. He had placed a single scarlet rose next to the freshly squeezed orange juice. There was a fresh peach, yoghurt with honey and toasted nuts, her favourite morning paper. The smell of freshly brewed coffee filled the room.

1

Ross tossed a bundle of envelopes onto the bed. 'Postman's just been. How's the gorgeous birthday girl?' he said. 'You don't look a day over twenty-five.'

'I *am* twenty-five, you fool.' She grinned. He could always make her laugh. And he had gone to some trouble to put all of her favourite things on the tray. She felt a rush of affection for him. I'm a selfish sod, she thought. I want it all – the fairy-tale, the lot.

Ross sat on the bed as she sipped her orange juice and opened her birthday cards. He looked handsome, having had his hair cut in a new, shorter style a few days ago. The spikiness suited his broad features and strong jaw. He was wearing a black denim shirt and jeans. Not the sort of clothes he usually favoured. Why the change? she wondered idly. He smiled, looking expectant.

'What?' she said.

'Did you think I'd forgotten your present? Look under the newspaper.'

Stacey looked at the slim black box, tied up with red ribbon. It would be chocolates, or a nightie, she thought, trying not to show her disappointment. But when she parted the layers of black tissue paper, she blinked in surprise. The pink rubber object was obviously some kind of sex toy. Slim straps were attached to the sturdy phallus and there was a strange appendage sticking out at a right-angle from the base of the shaft. She touched the oddly shaped wand. It was flat along one side and flexible.

'It's very . . . unusual,' she said, the corners of her mouth twitching. 'Whatever do you do with it?'

'Here. Let me show you,' Ross said, taking the tray and setting it on the floor.

Thinking that he was about to initiate some kind of sex, Stacey reached for him. Now you're talking, she thought, that's the kind of birthday present I want. But Ross had a strange look on his face. A new, steely glint in his eyes. She quickened with interest.

'Sit still. I'll put it on you,' he said. Stacey opened her mouth to protest, a giggle rising in her throat. 'Just – sit – still. Do as you're told for once. I mean it.' There was a hard edge to his voice.

Startled into obeying him, Stacey did as he asked. Ross folded back the bed-clothes and lifted the hem of her over-sized T-shirt. Stacey held up the garment as he instructed and looked down between her spread legs as Ross fitted on the contraption. She drew in her breath sharply as he lubricated the phallus and slipped it straight into her vagina. The thick stem felt intrusive, stretching open her entrance. She felt the urge to close her legs, but Ross's expression stopped her. He was totally absorbed in placing the flattened, flexible wand up the length of her sex, where it protruded slightly, the top of it veiled by her

3

pubic hair. Ross gently arranged her labia so that they pouted around the wand.

'Ross,' she began, 'I really don't think—'

'Shut up,' he said, without rancour. There was still that unfamiliar hardness to his voice.

Stacey felt a flicker of sexual arousal. Ross was behaving so strangely. She didn't know him in this mood. Now he was securing the straps around her waist, reaching to settle the other fastening between her legs. Finally he took from his pocket a tube of lubricating gel, squeezed a blob onto his fingertip and reached under the shaped wand that bisected her labia. The gel was cool against the tiny hood covering her clitoris.

'Stand up,' he said. 'Walk around. How does it feel?'

Stacey did as he ordered. It was quite a shock to feel the thick phallus buried within her. Her sex was held open by the girth of the rubber penis. As she moved, the referred, slippery pressure of the flattened wand made her clitoris erect. The tiny hood of flesh retracted and the little nub was forced against the shaped and lubricated strip. The friction was ticklish and quite maddeningly erotic.

'Well? How do you feel?' Ross said.

'Strange. Sort of sexy. A bit wicked and. . .'

'And? Go on. Tell me exactly.'

'Well. A bit . . . ashamed that it's turning me on, actually.' She searched for the right words. 'It's like a forbidden pleasure, because you can't tell

4

that I've got a big, thick cock right up inside my pussy.'

Ross's mouth lifted in a crooked grin. She could tell that he was excited by her directness. 'That's the idea. This is a training harness. It's designed to keep you aroused for hours. When you wear it to work today, only you and I will know what's going on inside your hot little knickers.'

Stacey's eyes opened wide in horror. 'You can't mean it! I'm not wearing this thing outside the house. No. Ross. Sorry. It's impossible.'

She moved to untie the straps, but realised that she was oddly reluctant to take the harness off. She couldn't wear it all day. Could she? The idea was preposterous, but oh-so intriguing.

Ross stayed her hand, saying sternly, 'Oh, but you will wear it, darling. In fact, you'll do exactly as I say. I want your word on this, Stacey. You won't remove it until I tell you to. And I insist that you don't relieve yourself. No nipping off to the cloakroom for a bit of sly masturbation!'

The very idea! How could he even suggest that she'd do such a thing? She found herself nodding mutely. 'All right,' she said at last in a low voice. To be truthful, she was more aroused than she had been in a very long time. She liked the new, masterful Ross. When he kissed her she responded eagerly, melding her tongue with his in a long explorative caress. When he drew back she was a little breathless, her face flushed.

'I haven't finished yet,' Ross said. 'There's

another part to your present.' He produced a tiny box which held two small silver rings. 'Take off your T-shirt.'

While Stacey stood with her hands by her sides, Ross pinched her nipples until they stood out firmly. Wetting them with spittle, he teased each of them in turn through the tightly fitting rings. The nipples, like hard shiny beads, pouted outwards into little tubes of collared flesh. Stacey winced at the intense, pinching pleasure. Her nipples seemed sensitised like never before.

Reaching into her lingerie drawer Ross extracted a pair of plain white cotton briefs and a matching bra. 'Put these on,' he said. 'Nice and functional. A perfect foil for what's underneath.'

Stacey did so. The training harness was almost invisible. Just the tiniest little bulge showed at the front of her panties where the flexible rod emerged from her sex-lips. She had a sudden thought. 'Oh, I haven't washed this morning. I'll have to take this all off.'

'No you won't. I want you to smell natural. You wash too often anyway. I'm always telling you how much I love the smell of your lovely pussy, but you ignore me.'

It was true. She could never believe he relished her rich, female muskiness. Usually she used the bidet twice a day, slipping into bed at night pristine and smelling of soap. Now she was forced to accept that Ross had told the truth when he complained that she tasted like a cosmetic factory. The thought of him waiting for her to come home so that he could enjoy her natural sexual odour was oddly exciting. Oh well, she thought, if it was good enough for Napoleon and Josephine. By the end of a busy day in the office she would be as spicy and earthy as Ross could wish for.

'By tonight you'll be begging for it, my darling,' Ross said. 'I'll think of you, aroused all day, but duty-bound to do nothing about it. Oh, if you need to pee, you'll find that you can bend the rod out of the way. Better hurry now. You'll be late. Wear something plain. A white, high-necked blouse and a black, knee-length skirt.'

Ten minutes later Stacey stood in the lift beside Ross as they descended to the car park below the block of flats. She sat gingerly on the car seat, but found that the training harness did not hamper her movements in any way. It was just that she was constantly aware of it. Just before they left Ross had put another smear of lubrication under the strip of rubber. She hardly needed it. Her natural lubrication was flowing freely. Inside the virginal cotton knickers, the shaped wand slipped and rubbed against her firmly erect clitoris, teasing her with a remorseless pressure.

'Bye, darling,' Ross said, drawing the car to a halt outside the Georgian-fronted building where Stacey worked for a firm of solicitors. 'Pick you up at the usual time. We'll go out for a meal straight after work. Okay? Have a good day.'

She waved and watched Ross drive away. It was something she rarely did. Today she waited until the car disappeared into the traffic before she went inside the building. She imagined Ross as he sat at his drawing board, working. The thought of her in the training harness would give him a prodigious erection. Somehow she knew that he was also pledged not to masturbate to relieve himself. As she went to the cloakroom and exchanged greetings with her colleagues, she could not stop thinking about Ross. And about the heightened state she would be in by the end of the day.

The working day seemed endless. It took all Stacey's efforts to concentrate on her work. Even the lunch party with close friends to celebrate her birthday was only a brief distraction. Her attention seemed centred in her groin and between her legs, where the stout rubber cock kept her swollen labia and vaginal entrance held open. She was acutely aware that she was made ready, available for sex, by the presence of the hideously arousing thing which was strapped to her body. The dichotomy of herself as coolly efficient legal secretary and wanton sex-object was a powerfully arousing concept. How the hell had Ross discovered that this was just what she needed?

By the afternoon, as she walked from her desk, returning tapes and legal documents to her boss's office, shivers of frustration were tickling down her thighs. The gusset of her panties was damp with her juices and there was a sense of heaviness, a delightful, engorged pressure, to her spread-open labia. Her clitoris felt as firm as a tiny cock under the oiled caress of the shaped wand. Her breasts were hard and swollen, the pulled-out tubes of her nipples rubbing deliciously against the cotton of her bra with every slight movement of her body. It was all she could do to sit still. Her fingers itched to plunge between her thighs. Just a few subtle movements and she would climax.

'Thank you, Stacey,' her boss said as she handed him a list of documents pertaining to a difficult client. 'That's a load off my mind.'

She smiled warmly. Mr Johnson was a senior partner in the firm. He was pushing fifty with a kind face and immaculate iron-grey hair. She knew that he found her attractive, although he would never step over the divide between them. If only he knew what was going on beneath her rather severe skirt and blouse!

Somehow Stacey kept her mind on her work, managing to complete the day with a minimum of mistakes. When she used the toilet she found that she could bend the wand away from her body. The phallus inside her exerted an inner pressure against her bladder, so that she had to urinate in a slow, steady stream. The accompanying tingle and sweet pulsing of her clitoris made even peeing a sensual act. She dabbed at herself with toilet tissue, cleaning herself carefully, hardly daring to brush against her ultra-eroticised pudenda. If she was to make herself come, even inadvertently, she would have to confess the fact to Ross.

It seemed that by wearing the harness she was made acutely aware of her whole body. The nipple rings inside her bra made her breasts almost unbearably sensitive. She stood well away from the other people in the lift on the way down, imagining that she might well reach orgasm if someone were to brush against the front of her blouse. But that did not happen and she was left wanting, teetering on the precipice of orgasm. By the time she was hurrying down the steps to the street towards Ross and the waiting car, she felt wrung out with tension and sheer physical longing. The whole of her sex felt hot and swampy.

'Had a good day, darling?' Ross said, his eyes gleaming wickedly.

She leaned over to kiss his cheek, wishing that he would turn his head and claim her mouth. 'What do you think?' she murmured.

As he edged the car into the flow of traffic, Ross gave a low chuckle. The sound of it seemed to hit her in the pit of the stomach.

'Let's not go out to eat,' Stacey said on impulse. 'Can't we go straight home?' Hitching up her skirt, she crossed her thighs suggestively.

He smiled and glanced across at her, then shook his head. ' 'Fraid not. The table's booked. The magic belt worked, I see. Well you'll just have to hold on a while longer.'

Tears of frustration gathered in Stacey's eyes. She had been kept at fever pitch for hours. Her nerves felt like brittle threads. 'You bastard,' she hissed. 'I'm dying for you. Don't you know that? But of course you do. That's the object of this exercise. I haven't been able to think of anything all day but what you'll do to me when we get back. Christ, I'm as horny as hell. My knickers are soaked.'

Ross kept his eyes on the road as he drove smoothly through the traffic. She could feel the sexual tension in every line of his body. God, had she really thought that he was unexciting? With his short, spiked hair and dark glasses, he looked unfamiliar, a little mysterious. She wanted him madly in a purely physical, utterly obscene way.

At the restaurant she drank a glass of wine and ate her artichoke vinaigrette in silence. Ross tapped her on the back of the hand and leaned close to hiss, 'Go and take off those prim white knickers. Raise your skirt when you come back so that your bare buttocks are resting against the wooden chair.'

Without a word she rose and did as he asked. Her pulses were racing. She always wore stockings, so when she returned and sat down she indeed felt the coolness of wood against her bottom. The hardness of the chair-seat pressed the phallus more deeply inside her. Somehow she ate the rest of her meal, hardly tasting the pasta

11

with saffron and cream sauce. Now and then Ross reached under the table to caress her naked thigh.

Once he reached between her legs to check the position of the instrument. She almost came when he ran a finger very lightly up the outside of the shaped wand and then gave her pouting labia an affectionate squeeze.

'You're really dying for it, aren't you? Tell me what you want,' Ross hissed in her ear. 'Tell me exactly what you want. I want to hear you talk dirty.'

While he sat back and ate his pasta, Stacey forced herself to give voice to her most private, wanton fantasies. Her cheeks burning, she said, 'I want your cock inside me. Hot and hard. No foreplay. Bloody hell, I've had a whole day of that. I want you to fuck my pussy while you suck my nipples and bite at the little rings . . .'

'And?' Ross said, his face impassive as he forked up the spicy tomato sauce.

'And . . . and . . . I want you to push a finger into my anus, while you suck my clitoris and lick up my juices. I want to make you come inside me.'

Stacey squirmed on the cool seat, pressing her pouting, thickened sex-lips against the now warm wood. Her juices had seeped down to pool on the chair. She could hardly believe she was saying these things. They usually didn't speak during sex. But that was then. Somehow this was now – a new time. A time of endless possibilities. Lord, what a birthday this was turning out to be!

Ross paid the bill while Stacey went to the cloakroom. She freshened her make-up and fluffed her short blonde hair, then studied her reflection. In the mirror she looked exactly as she always did. No one would guess that she was in such a state. On the way back to the flat, they did not speak. Ross ordered her to lift her skirt and open her legs wide, so that he could see the wand rudely bisecting her vulva.

'Stroke your pubes away from it. I want to see your pussy-lips,' he said.

Her face burning, Stacey used her fingers to part the damp hair. The inner surfaces of her labia were very red. They looked moist and fruity. She could smell herself – a rich, complex scent of aroused womanhood. All the way back she sat with her legs open, exposed to Ross's view, exposed in her own need.

As soon as they entered the flat, he took her in his arms and kissed her deeply. She responded with a desperate affection, hungry for his touch, his approval. Oh God, she loved him to distraction.

'Go upstairs,' he said. 'Raise your skirt and kneel at the end of the bed.'

Meekly she did so. It was a few minutes before he followed her. The bastard, he's making me wait, she thought as she pressed her thighs to the overhang of the duvet. She heard him come into the room, but did not look round. As he instructed, she made no move to help him when

13

he untied the straps at her waist. When he drew the phallus from her body, she gave a little cry of distress. It slipped wetly from between her puffy labia, a hot rush of body-warmed rubber.

Stacey surged against the bed, her hips pumping beyond her control. She felt faint with relief. After being held so open, made so aware that – in a purely sexual sense – she was simply an object in need of being filled, she experienced a curious sense of emptiness. But it lasted only seconds. Ross knelt behind her, his erect penis pressing urgently against her hungry sex.

Stacey chewed at her bottom lip as he pushed straight into her. He gripped her waist, drawing her back onto the full length of his rigid cock. Then he drove back and forth, pushing deeply, thrusting without gentleness. His hard stomach slapped against her buttocks. She felt his balls brushing against her as, with each inner stroke, the head of his cock stroked her sensitised cervix.

It was what she had craved all day. The muscular walls of her vagina spasmed around his shaft. Stacey thought she would faint. She screamed as she climaxed. The pleasure was mind-blowing, the contractions so intense that she sobbed and writhed, calling his name again and again.

'Oh, Ross. Christ, I love you. Ross. Oh, Ross.'

Ross withdrew. He flipped her over onto her back, tearing at her blouse buttons and dragging her bra away from her breasts. Holding a breast in

14

each hand, he held them up like offerings. As he mouthed her tormented nipples, his tongue flickering across the little rings, Stacey gasped and moaned. She was still hungry. Her thighs scissored around his slim hips as the pleasure prickled through her chest and down her belly. All she could think of was being penetrated again. But Ross drew away, slid down her body.

'This is what I've been anticipating,' he murmured.

He made little sounds of enjoyment as he feasted at her sex. His muscular tongue scooped up her juices, pushed into her vagina, lolled against her tingling clitoris. Gently he spread open her labia and licked the inner surfaces. Stacey climaxed again, turned on by Ross's own delight in her. When he moved back up to kiss her, she tasted her musk on his mouth.

As they locked together in an intensely erotic kiss, she lifted her thighs to welcome his cock back inside her. Now it was Ross who lost control. He bucked and surged against her, his slippery penis ramming into her again and again. Her ringed nipples were mashed against his muscular chest, the metal sliding on the thin film of sweat.

'Dear God. I can't . . .' she moaned. 'Oh yes, I can. I'm coming again.'

Incredibly Stacey felt herself building towards another peak. They climaxed together, laughing and crying at the same time. Ross held her tightly, like something unbearably precious.

It was some time before they could catch their breath. For a while they lay entwined, stroking each other in wonder and delight.

'How did you know?' Stacey whispered against Ross's mouth.

He grinned. 'Did you think you were the only one who was bored? Before we both succumbed to the seven-year itch I thought I'd find you a new man. Me. What's the verdict? Will I suit?'

'Oh, yes,' Stacey said happily. 'You'll do very well indeed. And I think you'll find you've got yourself a new woman!'

Julia's Burning

'THIS WAY, THE fire's through here. Oh, do hurry.' Julia clutched her long satin robe close, conscious that she wore only a few scraps of silk and lace beneath it.

'Stand back, madam,' the burly fireman said, putting out his arm to prevent her going back into the bedroom. 'I'll soon deal with this.'

She stood on the threshold, watching him as he crossed the room. In an instant he had quenched the fire. He turned and looked at her, a grin creasing his boyish face. Julia's pulses quickened. What a combination. That clean-cut face coupled with a big, obviously well-toned body was devastating.

'All done. Not much damage at all. Good thing you contacted us so quickly. Looks like an electrical fault. I'd advise you to have all the wiring checked.'

'Yes. Thanks. I will,' Julia said. 'I'm so grateful that you arrived promptly.'

'We were on our way back to the station. It's the end of my night shift.' He glanced at his wrist-watch. 'Actually I'm into free time now. My shift ended ten minutes ago.'

'Oh, I see,' Julia said, feeling guilty. 'Sorry for holding you up. I just panicked when that old electric heater started spurting flames. I suppose I could have tackled it myself . . .'

'No, you did right, madam. Best leave it to the experts.'

He smiled again and she felt a stab of heat in her belly. God, he was gorgeous. Those blue eyes and that firm, strong-looking mouth. The jacket of his uniform was open at the neck, showing an area of damp, honey-coloured skin. He seemed in no hurry to leave, despite being late already. In fact, the look in his eyes made her catch her breath.

'Would . . . would you like a drink?' she said. 'It's the least I can do to thank you for putting in overtime on my behalf.'

'Thought you'd never ask. Yeh, that'd be great. I'll just go down to the lads and tell them to go back to the station without me.'

When he left the room Julia hurried over to a pine dresser and looked in the mirror. She used her fingers to muss her hair and sprayed herself with perfume. Her eyes and cheeks glowed. She knew that she looked good. She wasn't pretty,

18

exactly, but the combination of her red-brown hair and pale skin gave her a definite allure. Besides, what she lost in fashionable features, she made up for in lush curves. She was quite proud of her unfashionable, hour-glass figure. She might not be model-girl material, but men found her a big turn-on.

Before she left the bedroom, she adjusted the neck of the satin robe so that it showed off her creamy chest and the deep valley of her breasts. As she descended the stairs, the fireman was closing the front door. There was another man with him. He turned and gave Julia a frankly appraising look. Her heart almost skipped a beat. Two of them – identical twins.

'Hope you don't mind if my brother joins us,' the first fireman grinned. 'We do everything together. By the way, I'm Tony and this is Max. If you object we'll leave. No problem.'

They seemed to fill the hall with their presence. The big uniformed bodies ought to have been intimidating, but Julia felt wildly aroused. She sensed no menace from them, only a sort of contained tension.

'Double trouble, eh?' she said. 'I think I can handle that.' This couldn't be happening. It was like a scene from a film. 'Come into the kitchen. I'll make tea.'

She almost laughed at herself. How English to offer tea! So much for her efforts to act cool.

'Tea's fine for me,' said Tony, gazing admiringly

at her cleavage and nipped-in waist. Max said, 'Me too. Have you got something to spike it with?'

While the men sat at the kitchen table, Julia filled the kettle, set out cups and took a bottle of whisky from a cupboard. They made small talk and Julia responded, but all the time she was aware of the potent male presence of the uniformed figures. The fire-proof jackets and trousers, the buckled webbing belts with attached instruments and the stiff gauntlets lying on the table seemed dangerous and incongruous in her neat, bright kitchen.

She poured tea with trembling hands, adding a generous tot of whisky to each cup. Even with her back turned she was conscious of their hot eyes on her as she moved. The satin clung to the rich curve of her bottom, the indentation of her waist. Her breasts seemed swollen, the erect nipples scraping deliciously against the lace of her bra. She felt herself getting wet between her legs.

'Thanks,' Tony said, accepting a cup of tea. Max grinned up at her as she leaned over to set a cup down beside him. He was not identical to his twin after all. His face was more angular, his jaw squarer. But his eyes were just as blue. There was a wicked, knowing gleam in them. A frank and unashamed sexuality. This man was a bit of a rogue.

It seemed that something clutched at Julia's womb. The rush of heat to her loins shocked her.

She was standing next to Max, her satin-clad thigh almost touching his protective trousers. As she went to turn away, he reached out a hand and grasped the belt at her waist. Julia did not pull away as he drew one hand down her satin-covered flank.

'Seems to me that there's another fire here for us to deal with, bro,' Max said. He winked at Tony. 'The lady's sorely in need of our expert attentions.'

Julia closed her eyes as the belt slithered to the floor and Max's hands closed on her waist. She hardly dared believe that this was happening. Her fantasy was going to come true. Max stroked her soft belly, reached up to feel her breasts, and then slid a hand down to cup her lace-covered pubis. One fingertip scratched lightly at the fabric triangle, scoring the slight indentation between her labia.

Julia felt her knees grow weak as he handled her. His touch was gentle, but proprietorial. Tony watched, a crooked grin on his mouth as his twin teased and aroused her. She swayed towards him, wishing that he would reach for her too. Max slid two fingers inside her panties, meshed them in the luxuriant bush of her pubic hair. Julia squirmed as he twirled the hair, stroking it away from her heated centre, but holding back from touching her slippery folds. God, how she wished he would touch her clitoris. It was throbbing and ticking with a life of its own.

'You know, Max,' Tony said, 'seems to me that we've been brought here under false pretences. There ought to be a penalty for wasting our valuable time.'

'Yeh,' Max said. 'You're so right, bro. What shall we do with you, Julia? You're guilty of wrongful use of council services. That's a serious matter. I'm afraid a cup of tea spiked with whisky just doesn't cut it.'

'I'm . . . I'm sorry,' Julia said lamely, trembling as his hands moved upwards now to grasp the cups of her bra.

'Oh, you will be,' Max said with a wolfish grin. With a swift movement he dragged her breasts free so that the full globes and dark nipples were exposed. Lifted by the cups and resting on the rim of boned fabric beneath them, her generous breasts were thrust into lewd prominence.

Julia made a tiny sound of distress deep in her throat as a blissful rush of shame swept her whole body. Tony now reached out his hand and slipped it into the top of her lace panties. He dipped between her legs, parted her labia, and slid one finger into her. 'Mmm. She's nice and wet. And look at those firm teats. Seems like she's expecting something.'

'Then we ought not to disappoint the lady,' Max said.

Julia couldn't speak for the desire which was like a burning presence in the whole area below her waist. When Tony withdrew his hand and

22

stood up, she made no sound. Her legs seemed to have turned to water. When Max also rose, gripped her hips and pushed her belly down onto the kitchen table she gave a muffled protest. Her bare breasts were pressed against the cool wood. The sensation on her erect nipples was startlingly erotic.

'Now then, Julia. Time to take your punishment,' Tony said, raising the hem of the satin robe and tucking it into the band of her suspender belt in the small of her back.

Julia's cheeks flamed as Max dragged down her panties and left them cuffed beneath the underswell of her buttocks. He exerted a gentle pressure so that she was pushed further onto the table. Her stockinged feet slipped on the tiled floor and her legs splayed lewdly outwards. She imagined how she must look, her hair spilling over her face, her breasts exposed, and her big bare bottom sticking in the air. Her sex was clearly visible between her parted thighs, the wet red lips peeping through the luxurious red-brown hair. Oh Lord, it was so arousing to have both men desiring her.

'Nice arse,' Tony said. 'A bit too pale though. Have to remedy that.'

Julia bit her lip as the first open-handed slap landed squarely on her right buttock. She had gathered herself to meet the pain, but she was so worked up it felt more like a rough caress. So this was to be her punishment. But could it really be called that if she enjoyed it? And she was loving every minute of it. While Tony spanked her right buttock, now and then stopping to circle the blushing flesh with a soothing palm, Max gave his full attention to the left.

She moaned and writhed with the stinging pleasure, feeling the wetness pool between her legs. How awful if she oozed onto the table. They would both see what a hussy she was. When her bottom was glowing, the spanking stopped. Julia was almost disappointed. She had liked the feel of both men handling her.

Tony reached underneath her and grasped her breasts. Kneading them, he circled the turgid nipples with his thumb. Julia held her breath. Her nipples were dark and prominent. She loved having them pinched. Another trickle of warm juice dripped from inside her. If Tony kept on doing that, she was going to climax.

Then something hard and cold was placed between her thighs. Julia jerked with shock and turned her head to see that Max had taken his fireman's axe from his belt. It was the stout rubber handle she could feel. It pressed against her soaking vulva, the domed tip brushing firmly against her clitoris.

Of their own volition her hips began to weave. She arched her back, pushing out her simmering bottom, spreading her legs wider, straining them apart, as the axe handle moved towards her hungry vagina. It circled the orifice, the tip edging inside her, but not going in very far. Julia almost wept with frustration as Max and Tony teased her. She was sure that her syrupy juices must be trickling down the handle. The prickling throbbing of her nipples was maddening, echoing the thrumming of her stiff little clit.

'Hot little piece, isn't she?' Max said huskily. 'I think she's ready to be quenched. You first?'

'After you, bro,' Tony said gallantly.

The way they spoke about her, almost dismissively but with obvious admiration, drove Julia wild. They seemed used to sharing women and the thought made her eager for whatever they offered. When Max opened the buttons on his flame-proof trousers, she leaned towards him, eager to watch his cock spring free. The bulge tenting his underwear held great promise. She just knew that his member would be thick and veiny. Just the sort of cock she liked.

Max didn't take down his trousers, he just reached a hand in and drew out his penis. Julia licked her lips. It was just as she'd imagined. A flushed, robust stem, rising from a thatch of light-brown pubes. Not over-long, but thick and with a big shiny glans. Somehow seeing it sticking out of his uniform, collared by the open fly of his white boxers, was more exciting than seeing him naked.

Max put a hand on the back of her head, but she needed no urging to take him into her mouth. He was hot and tasted gamey. She smelled sweat and rubber, and something vaguely chemical from his uniform. Running her tongue down his length, she worked her mouth back and forth, sucking and spreading spittle along his length. Max grunted and stroked her face, meshing his fingers in her silky hair.

Julia became aware that Tony had moved between her thighs. His fingers were on her sex, spreading her swollen labia, fluttering over her inner folds. She imagined him looking down at her exposed sex and bucked as his hands brushed against her mildly sore buttocks, eager for the penetration that was to come. Tony pushed two fingers inside her while his thumb spread her juices upwards then gently circled her anus.

With his other hand Tony spread her buttocks apart until the tight, puckered orifice was lewdly stretched open. She steeled herself for the insertion of his thumb. As he pushed it into her, she cried out at the unfamiliar invasion. The base of his thumb was wedged up hard against the inner surface. With both Tony's fingers and thumb buried deeply inside her pulsing flesh, she began sobbing and working her hips in a shameless display of lust.

It was almost unbearably erotic to be manhandled in this way. Filled in three places at once, Julia felt the pressure of a climax building.

Max thrust into her willing mouth, his firm scrotum brushing against her chin. A drop of salty liquid slid on her tongue. He was near to orgasm. She rammed down onto him, relaxing her throat so that she could embrace the full length of him. With a gasp Max went rigid. His cock spasmed as his come jetted into her throat. At the same time Tony's clever fingers drew down the pleasure from her body. The subtle internal stroking behind her pubic bone, coupled with the meeting of his thumb through the thin membrane, tipped her over.

As she swallowed Max's come, the first ripples of her orgasm broke over her. Her vagina tightened around Tony's fingers, dry-milking him as she moaned with pleasure. She moved against his hand, grinding herself against his knuckles, wanting something, anything, everything. When the fingers and thumb were withdrawn she cried out with disappointment.

Tony chuckled as he opened his fly and fitted on a ridged condom. 'This fire takes some putting out! Good thing we're well equipped.'

Max moved away, tucking his softening cock back into his boxers. He bent and kissed Julia on the forehead. 'Don't worry,' he grinned. 'My bro's up to coping with any blaze.'

Then Julia felt herself filled by the full length of Tony's erect, covered penis. She was so wet and swollen inside that the slightest movement sent exquisite sensations raging through her pelvis. As he pounded into her, her upper body was pressed against the table. Her breasts lolled to the sides, the sensitive nipples chafing against the smooth, cool wood. As another climax built inside her, she lifted her bottom, loving the soft scrape of Tony's pubic hair against her sensitised buttocks.

'Christ!' Tony grunted. 'Oh, yeh. Oh, man.'

His pelvis rammed up tight against her as he emptied himself into the condom. Breathing hard, he bent over her, taking his weight on his hands, while the contractions of her vagina bled him of every last drop of pleasure. It was a moment before either of them could move. Julia was vaguely conscious of Max moving around the kitchen as, slowly, Tony withdrew. He bent and dropped a kiss on each scarlet buttock.

'Stay as you are,' he said. 'Max will see to the clean-up job.'

Julia relaxed as Max wiped her from front to back with a piece of kitchen roll. Then she rose unsteadily, pulled up her panties, and adjusted her bra. Her cheeks were as red as her buttocks. She could hardly bear to meet their eyes.

Tony and Max took their places at the table as if nothing had happened. Max picked up his cup, took a sip and screwed up his face. 'Ugh, tea's gone cold. It's not bad though, with the whisky.'

Julia smiled openly then. 'I'll make some fresh. And how about the usual? Scrambled eggs, bacon, mushrooms, beans, toast suit you? Can't have my two favourite firemen falling down on the job through lack of energy!'

Tony and Max laughed. 'If this was more than a once-a-month arrangement, we might need an energy transplant!' Tony said.

Julia gathered together the ingredients to make breakfast. 'Just you relax, boys. Your room's ready upstairs. After you've eaten you can sleep for a while. Then I think you'll find I've another fire for you to deal with – before your next shift!'

Looking-Glass

'WHERE'D YOU WANT it, love?'

Looking at the mirror again Josie wondered what had possessed her to buy it. Still, it had been a bargain for fifty quid. With that ornate gilt frame, all garlands, swags and cherubs, it had to be at least a hundred years old. It was so imposing, so ugly, that no one else had wanted it.

Josie had found herself bidding when the price dropped. Somehow she had known that it was meant for her.

'Well?' the delivery man said, losing patience. 'I haven't got all day. Which room? Up or down?'

For a moment Josie was nonplussed. She had not thought that far ahead. What was wrong with her? She was not given to making impulsive purchases. In fact, she was not impulsive at all – usually. It seemed to her then that she heard Sam's voice – his tone of bored annoyance, one she remembered only too well.

'Where the hell did you get that monstrosity? Are you mad?'

That decided it. She felt a surge of mild rebellion. I'll do as I damn well like, she thought.

'It can go in the bedroom,' she told the delivery man, who was still struggling to negotiate the front door. 'Upstairs on the right. Lean it against the end wall, in the alcove.'

The room was all hers now, since Sam had walked out on her. For the promise of an extra tenner, the delivery man was persuaded to help her hang the mirror. An hour later it looked down on her bed, adding light and space to the alcove. It would look better after she had cleaned it. She took a step back, rubbing at a spot on the glass with the cuff of her cotton sweatshirt. Her reflection stared back at her.

Not bad-looking. Dark blonde hair, longish face. Not exactly pretty, but striking, and she had good bones. Curious how light played tricks on glass. She could have sworn she saw a movement in the green-tinged depths.

Yes. There it was. A pale area – roughly oval. It came more clearly into focus the more she stared at it. A chill ran down her back. The shape looked like a face. She rubbed her eyes, looking again. Nothing. The misty, oval shape had gone. Josie's heart skipped back to its normal rhythm.

Sam would have said that she had been reading too many of her 'weird' books, as he called them.

31

That was another thing they had disagreed on. She had told him that 'occult' only meant hidden knowledge – the unknown – but he had not approved of her choice of reading material.

'Why can't you read romantic novels or sex-and-shopping, like normal women?' he had said contemptuously. 'Instead of all that bloody rubbish about ghosts and ghouls.'

She smiled wanly now, not surprised that she was seeing things. She knew that she was over-tired, tense. The doctor told her she was suffering from stress – the twentieth-century disease. Hardly surprising. It was only two months since the divorce had become final.

Roy, her best friend and owner of the antique shop where she worked, had suggested a simple solution.

'Go out and get yourself laid, love. Take two weeks off. It's our quiet time. Get away somewhere where there's sun and sand. You need a new man. Take it from me. It's a tried and tested cure.'

'Maybe for you, you old queen,' Josie said in a teasing voice.

Roy struck a pose. 'Dearie me! What's sauce for the goose, you know!'

She had taken the time off, but not the holiday. It was too soon. Sam had done a really good job on her. In his eyes she rated about as highly as an insect, when compared with his new love – a luscious brunette with money to back up her over-active libido. Trouble was, Sam's opinion seemed to have rubbed off on her. In a few months maybe she would be ready for 'walking on the beaches, looking at the peaches', as Roy would sing.

Right now she felt like getting blind drunk. Thinking of Sam had that effect on her.

Josie took the bottle of brandy to bed with her. For a while she watched TV. The brandy and the re-run of one of her favourite films, 'Someone to Watch Over Me', relaxed her. When the film ended, she switched off the TV. Stretching out, still fully dressed, she leafed through a raunchy magazine – another of Roy's smart ideas. 'You can weigh up the talent,' he said with a laugh. 'You have to admit you're out of touch, love. What with having been married to a dinosaur for so long!'

The centrefold was a blond, beach-bum type, with a come-hither expression and a body to die for. Josie ran the pad of her thumb over his taut stomach and up over the prominent pectorals. Dipping down to the groin, she dragged her nails over the cock and balls. Shame he was not erect. It seemed stupid that all naked men in women's magazines were obliged to sport flaccid cocks. It wasn't exactly the greatest turn-on.

Still, something worked. Perhaps it was the beach boy's expression – macho but sort of 'I've got a soft centre'. Whatever, Josie felt a stir of interest. Roy was right. She did need a man in her life. Someone who fancied her madly, who would spread her out on the bed, kiss her all over, and tell her that she was the most fuckable woman in the world.

Trouble was, she was not ready for all the stuff that went with it. And for Josie, sex without a close relationship just didn't work. She was too hooked on commitment. Oh well, I suppose I'm going to have to face up to being lonely for a while, she thought resignedly, taking another swallow of brandy. She felt pleasantly woozy. There was an unfamiliar heaviness in her pussy, a slickness when she moved her legs. It had been a long time since she felt the urge to masturbate. Well, why the hell not. She deserved some pleasure, solitary or otherwise.

She fetched the vibrator she had bought at an Anne Summers party and settled back on the bed. The vibrator had been another impulse buy, she realised, a joke. She had never yet used it. It was made of some transparent pink material and had a plastic bubble, filled with little round beads, set partway down the shaft.

Reaching down, Josie unzipped her jeans and eased them down her legs. Sliding her thumbs into the waistband of her cotton lace pants, she took those off too. The sight of her reflection in the new mirror aroused her further. She looked wanton and sexy, naked from the waist down and with her hair all mussed. Her eyes glowed with a brandy-lent flame.

She still could not work out why she had bought the mirror, but it seemed like a better idea with each passing moment. She had never watched herself masturbate before. This would be a first. 'The start of a new Josie,' she slurred happily. 'Are you watching me, mirror?'

As she moved her hand down over her stomach, a feeling of warm tension spread around her pussy. She raised her legs and let her knees fall open, watching as the outer lips spread and the pink inner surfaces of her labia were revealed. Already they were glistening with juices. The opening to her vagina was a dark and mysterious shadow. It looked like velvet. Something about the mirror enhanced the look of her. Was her skin really that texture – like thick cream? And did her hair always have that sheen?

'Eat your heart out, Sam. You bastard. This is your loss!' she said aloud on a laugh.

Who needed him anyway? Josie shuddered with pleasure as she took in her enhanced mirror-image. God, she looked really sexy. She watched as her fingers spread her inner lips open more widely and began playing up and down the moist slit. Little ripples of sensation spread down to her thighs. She decided to put off using the vibrator for a while; save it as a treat, play with herself while savouring the thought of it.

She gave a little purr of pleasure. This was somehow more intimate than fucking. You could be making love with someone and not quite lose

35

yourself. The other person claims so much of you, she thought, yet *you* feel guilty if they don't make you come. Self-love was entirely voluptuous. The selfishness of it was what appealed. Funny that she had never allowed Sam to watch her do this to herself. She was glad of that now. This act was hers alone. Let him pork that fat, brown-haired bimbo he had run off with! She didn't care any more.

There seemed to be a secret complicity between herself and the greenish glass reflection. Her hand worked faster, three wet fingers lightly circling her clit, varying the pressure. Slowly, teasing herself with the image and the reality, she inserted the tip of one finger into her vagina. Her mirror image did the same. How shiny her finger looked, how reluctant the slick pink flesh was to release it.

As Josie lifted her hips, flexing her knees and thrusting her belly upwards, the image in the mirror wavered. A flicker of light passed across the glass surface. Josie was too engrossed to notice for a moment. She strained her legs wide, opening her buttocks to reveal the tight rose-shape of her anus. It was moist, ringed with a few dark blond curls.

She tickled the little mouth with the tips of two fingers. It seemed a naughty, forbidden act. Never had she felt so wanton, so down-to-earth sexual. Her clitoris burned and throbbed as she stroked it. She smeared the juice seeping from her vagina all over her deliciously swollen pussy. Wetting her forefinger, she slipped it a little way inside her anus. There was some resistance at the entrance, then a feeling of acceptance as she pressed gently but remorselessly inwards. It felt like hot silk in there.

Oooooh, how naughty. Another first. Josie, you bad girl.

She pushed the finger all the way into her bottom, gasping at the mixed sensations that flooded her belly. In the mirror she looked wild. Her eyes glowed with a peculiar lambency as her body twisted and bucked. She could not look away from the delightful lewdness of the image. Her legs spread in wild abandonment, her pussy wet and glistening. Her fingers thrust inside her body, working and working to bring her to a sweet release.

Oh, it was magic or Heaven or both.

Pausing for a moment to reach for the vibrator, she twisted the base to turn it on. The low deep humming caused her pussy to throb with anticipation. As she caressed her soaking flesh with the bright pink phallus she shivered all over with a singular pleasure. On the brink of coming, she plunged the vibrator into her vagina. The feel of the clear bubble containing all the little buzzing, rotating beads drove her wild. Her hips wove madly as her orgasm rolled over her. She screamed and bit her lips, exulting in the sound she made, letting out all the grunts and groans of pleasure which she had kept caged from Sam. Her internal pulsings were deep and satisfying and seemed to go on and on.

When they faded, finally, she slumped back in exhaustion, replete as never before. In a while, she wiped herself with a tissue, cleaned the vibrator and put it away. Pouring herself another generous measure of brandy, she held up the glass to the mirror. 'Here's to plenty more shared good times,' she said with a wide grin. 'Mirror, mirror on the wall. You're a beauty – the best partner of all!'

She knocked the brandy back, then looked at the mirror in puzzlement. Pushing herself upright, she peered closely at the surface. There seemed to be a large smear on the glass. Head swimming with the after-glow of the brandy and the orgasm, she reached behind her for something to rub the mirror with. Her fingers closed over the damp tissue.

She rubbed at the patch and the glass came clean. It was only dust after all. Realising what she had used to wipe the mirror, she giggled. 'Oops, sorry, mirror. I've just smeared you with pussy juice! Hope you don't mind!'

The room spun around her. Josie fell back onto the bed, still laughing softly. She felt happy, carefree for the first time in many weeks. Groggily, she pulled off the rest of her clothes and dropped them onto the bedroom carpet. Flopping onto the pillows, she closed her eyes. Warm, relaxed, and sated, she fell asleep.

An hour later Josie awoke. Feeling cold, she sat up to pull the duvet over herself. Moonlight flooded the room through the slats in the Venetian blinds. The surface of the mirror looked silvery, as if it had absorbed every ray of light that penetrated the room.

She could see the clean spot where she had wiped the layer of dust with the tissue. Her eyelids drooped, then snapped open. The clean patch on the mirror was . . . glowing. Impossible. It could not be. But it was.

Josie watched with a mixture of fascination and horror. The clean spot was definitely getting bigger. Before her eyes the edges of the smudge pushed outwards. As it grew, the light followed it. Josie did not dare to move. Perhaps it was a brandy-induced dream. No. She was awake – muzzy-headed, but fully conscious. The glow was still growing. Finally it spread all over the surface of the mirror. There was a new depth inside the sumptuous frame. Josie could see right *inside* the mirror.

At first there was only a blank sheet of light, then the image condensed, sharpened. Josie swallowed audibly, finding herself gazing into a room. It seemed to be a boudoir. Red flocked paper covered the walls. There was a mahogany dressing-table with a mirror, a lacquered screen in one corner. Fringed velvet curtains masked the windows. The soft glow of an oil lamp illuminated the room. To one side there was a chaise longue.

Then the door opened and a woman stepped into the mirror-room.

She had thick red hair, a striking, longish face. Her hair was pinned up, leaving her slender neck bare. A froth of red curls framed her forehead. She wore a robe that had a deep collar of lace threaded with silk ribbons. Around her neck was a velvet choker with a cameo.

Josie was transfixed. More unexpected than anything that had happened so far was the fact that the woman had her face.

'My God. It's me. It's really me,' Josie breathed. 'I'm in the mirror. But it's a different me.'

She looked down, felt her limbs, pinched herself. Solid enough, real. Then it must be an image of herself she was looking at. She had read about doppelgängers. Was it possible? The fact that she felt no menace whatsoever stopped her from flinging herself off the bed and fleeing the room. Nothing but benevolence came from the mirror and its image.

Sitting sideways on to Josie, the mirror-woman patted her abundant red hair, tweaking the frothy curls at the front into shape. She bit her lips to make them full and red, then picked up a cut-glass scent bottle. Removing the stopper, she used it to apply perfume to her pulse points – behind her ears, in the crook of her elbow, on the insides of her wrists. Josie smelled the lavender and heliotrope notes of 'Jicky', her own favourite classic French perfume. With a mischievous smile the mirror-woman shrugged off the robe and applied a dab of perfume between her breasts.

Josie's pulses quickened. Her fear was fast fading and an unwilling fascination was taking over. The sheer natural sensuality of her other self exerted a powerful pull on her senses. The red-haired woman was obviously expecting a lover. And the glimpse of those full breasts jutting over the top of a tightly-laced corset sent a dart straight to Josie's stomach.

How pretty the clothes were, all those frills and flounces. She would like to wear things like that. It was Sam who had preferred her to wear tight jeans and clinging T-shirts. She wondered now why she had gone on wearing them. They were not even comfortable. She watched her alter-ego in the mirror, held by the spell of her. The woman looked innocent, but knowing at the same time. Do I look like that? Josie wondered.

The woman smoothed her black stockings up over shapely ankles, securing them behind her knees with frilled garters. Loose-legged, frilled drawers reached to her knees, only partly concealing the swell of her hips. The drawers were made of some thin stuff. Josie could see the faint shadow of hair on the woman's pubic mound. She turned now and bent to pick up the discarded robe and her drawers stretched tautly across her rounded bottom. Josie saw the indentation that marked the parting between the woman's full cheeks.

She could not help but admire the lushness of the figure before her. Sam had insisted that Josie dieted. Fool that she was, she had complied. Her body was angular now, her breasts almost flat, and her hips bordering on the boyish. She had the body that Sam wanted. Yet he had run off with the buxom brunette.

The woman in the mirror is me as I ought to be, she realised.

A new excitement gripped her as she saw that the scene in the mirror was changing. A door opened and a man walked into the boudoir. No words passed between the two figures, yet Josie was certain that the man and woman were on intimate terms.

The man was tall, broad-shouldered, blond. In fact, he looked rather like the pin-up in the magazine, which lay discarded amongst the rumpled bedclothes. The woman stood up and faced the man. Smiling slightly, she raised one leg and rested it on the stool, then began to fiddle with the toe of her stocking. The man said nothing, his eyes drawn to the drawers she wore. Because of her lifted leg he could see they were open at the crotch. The opening gaped, giving him a view of rounded thighs and the plump sex nestling between them.

One of the woman's hands strayed to her exposed thigh, stroking it gently, describing small circles on the creamy skin. Glancing up from lowered lashes, she gave the man a look of arch invitation. 'Shall I?' she seemed to be asking him.

'Yes. Oh, yes,' Josie breathed, lost in the sensuality of the scene as her alter-ego's finger toyed with her pubic curls before slipping into her parted slit. She's playing with him, teasing him, Josie thought. She had never had the confidence or the desire to do that to Sam.

The mirror-woman parted her legs and opened the lips of her sex with two fingers, exerting an upwards pressure so that her clitoris stood proud of the surrounding folds. At the expression on the man's face, Josie felt a tingle go right through her. The reddish hair on the woman's vulva glistened in the lamp-light. Her held-open labia looked swollen as if pouting and the man had a clear view of the moist inner flesh. Around the woman's vagina the flesh was a deeper red.

Josie licked her lips nervously. She would never dare to act that way. But her other self was totally at ease with her femininity. She really likes herself, Josie realised, while I never have.

The mirror-woman opened her thighs wide, letting the bent leg fall to one side. The man wore an avid expression. He looked as if he longed to press his mouth to that tender crevice, to suckle the flesh-hood and draw the nub of the clitoris into the curl of his tongue. He looked as if he wanted to drink her juices, smell the rich musk, to hear the woman sigh and moan under him.

Josie needed a man to want *her* like that. A good-looking man, strong yet sensitive. A man just like the one in the mirror. She found herself moving down the bed, nearing the frame that surrounded the intimate tableau. In a daze of arousal and need, Josie moved closer until she was looking directly into the mirror. The glass seemed to have melted. It had ceased to be a barrier. Surely it was a doorway.

Too late now for doubt or wonderment. Somehow Josie knew that if she refused to accept it was impossible, then it became reality. Reaching out her hand, she stretched her whole body towards the man. Without any apparent change of perception, she found herself looking directly up at him. She was conscious that she had one foot resting on a stool. From the corner of her eye she saw the lacquered screen and the lamp.

'I've been waiting for you a long time,' the man said, his intense blue eyes glittering.

Josie's heart turned over. The man's wide, sensual mouth curved in a smile of welcome. In that smile there was kindness, humour, and recognition. For a moment she was dizzy. But his hand in hers was strong, solid. Real. The chemise and drawers, the corset, felt strange and yet so familiar, so right.

Unable to resist, she turned and looked in the large ornate mirror which hung on the wall behind her. Do I still exist in the real world? she thought. With relief she saw the bedroom with its slatted blinds. In it she saw a thin, fair-haired woman sitting on a rumpled bed, a crumpled magazine beside her. She looked so unhappy that Josie felt sorry for her.

The man, her perfect lover, embraced the mirror-Josie. He ran his hands over her waist, stroked the rich swell of her hips. He smoothed the cambric drawers against her skin, hooking his fingers into the deep valley that bisected her generous rump. What was his name? It did not matter. It was what he represented that was important. Absorbing the truth of this, Josie gave a husky laugh and unlaced the front of her chemise, slipping the lacy neckline off her shoulders.

Her lover groaned as she freed her breasts and allowed them to fall forward. His mouth quested into the perfumed cleavage. He pressed kisses to the firm flesh, seeking a hold on a nipple. Josie sighed when he drew her nipple into his mouth and began lashing it with his tongue. After a moment he drew back and gazed admiringly at the full globes, the large, pale-pink buds.

Josie felt the urge to laugh with sheer happiness. 'You're perfect. The perfect lover.'

Her lover stroked her forehead, smoothing back the curls. 'I am for you, my darling,' he said softly.

An ache built within Josie. Her sex seemed actually to throb with lustful heat. Oh God, she needed desperately for him to bury himself in her liquid warmth. Her eyes met his. He seemed to know what she wanted. In a moment he had turned her around, bent her forwards over the broad stool. The drawers gaped open around her bottom. She smelled the sweet pungent musk of her own arousal. Then she was sinking back onto him, guiding the head of his cock into the tight purse of her sex. His flesh filled her, the stout head forging into her molten core.

She felt him shudder as he moved inside her, slowly at first, rimming her opening with the fat glans. Josie slammed her buttocks against the base of his hard belly, knowing that he felt the strong squeeze of her flesh-walls. Her lover cried out as he buried his shaft deep inside her, moving in time with her breathy moans.

'Do it to me, my darling girl,' he murmured. 'Milk me of my jism. Make me pant. Make me spend.'

The old-fashioned terms spurred Josie on. The cock leapt and twitched inside her. Never before had she felt such an all-consuming lust. His pubic hair ground against her bottom as Josie sighed and writhed on him. Moving her hand to the gap in her drawers, she rubbed herself as he pounded into her.

She could see their reflection in the large wall mirror – for mirror it had become again. The open drawers gave her a full view of her juicy quim, stretched wide around her lover's thick stem. She was wet and slick as a seal. Josie drank in the sight of her strong back; the perfect heart-shape of her generous, spread buttocks; the crumpled anus, pushed out slightly by the pressure of the rampant cock inside her; her sturdy thighs which took her lover's weight easily.

She loved herself like this, with rounded limbs and fat on her bones. How secure she felt, within the cushioning expanse of flesh.

'Oh, I'm spending. Oh Lord,' her lover cried.

Josie came too, the ripples of her contracting quim drawing the sperm from him. As her lover spasmed and emptied himself, her entire body tingled with the ecstasy of total release. She forgot Sam, the erosion of her self-confidence, the messy divorce, the long lonely nights. She forgot about Roy's advice and the fact that things like this could not happen. She believed. Let cynics like Sam hold on to their views if they wanted to.

Her lover kissed her gently before he left. 'I'm always here for you,' he whispered against her mouth.

Josie cupped his face in her hands and murmured, 'Thank you, for more than you realise.'

When he had gone, she looked into the mirror and saw again the image of the thin blonde woman on the bed. Moonlight crept in through the slatted blind. The other Josie was sleeping now, a smile on her untroubled face. The mirror-Josie knew that she must go back and enter the body of the woman on the bed, but that her alter-ego would always exist within the mirror. Her lover waited there too.

As she moved towards the mirror, the image of the boudoir behind her wavered and grew dark. She found herself looking down on her sleeping self and smelled the familiar odour of clean bed-linen and new paint. Then her cheek was resting against the cool pillowcase and all was peaceful.

In the mirror, the red-haired woman smiled tenderly. The lamp flickered and went out.

In the modern bedroom, the moonlight glimmered on a solid sheet of greenish glass.

Succubus

ROSE GAVE EMMA a lingering kiss, then fitted the key into the ornate front door.

'See you in the morning then?' she said, hoping that Emma would change her mind and stay in the house with her.

Emma shuddered and pulled up the collar of her black leather jacket. She looked up at the pointed-arch windows that seemed to stare down at the two women.

'It's a bloody mausoleum. I've always hated this house.' Her voice softened, became wheedling. She reached up to stroke Rose's cheek. 'You don't have to do this, you know. Come back to the flat with me.'

Rose grinned, enlivening her elfin face. 'I never go back on a dare. You should know that by now.'

'I won't hold you to it. We were both drunk. What is it with you and this house, anyway?'

Rose shrugged, the mass of striking red dreadlocks dancing around her shoulders. She opened the front door. 'You keeping me company or what?'

Emma's straight brows dipped in a frown. 'Sod you then, if you won't listen to sense. I'm off.'

She turned with a flick of her short black skirt, Doc Marten boots scuffing through the wet leaves that clotted the brick path. Rose watched her go, thinking that even now Emma might change her mind. She was not usually so stubborn. But Emma did not turn around. As her lover banged the wrought-iron gate shut behind her, Rose stepped through the front door.

Late afternoon sun streamed through the stained-glass door panel, casting coloured diamonds onto the floor tiles. The house smelled musty, sweetish, with the faintest trace of old lavender polish. Rose smiled, recalling childhood memories of visiting her grandmother. Gran's house had smelt just like this. It was a shame that Emma was still spooked by unpleasant memories of her dotty aunt. Anyone could see that the house was a gem. It belonged to the living. How could Emma even consider selling it?

She climbed the stairs, trailing her fingers along the carved bannisters, feeling the coldness of the wood under her palms. On her back was a holdall containing candles, food, incense sticks, a flask of coffee. Got to do this right.

Dust sheets covered the furniture. The rooms

seemed filled with white, lumpy shapes, iced rocks in the gloom. Nothing had been touched since the old lady's death. Somehow the house had escaped the notice of vandals and squatters. Odd, in this area, to see the red brick walls free from graffiti. Did everyone believe the ghost stories?

Rose made herself comfortable in one of the bedrooms. Maroon velvet curtains hung at either side of the window. More of the same fabric, this time swagged and threaded with gold cord, hung over the bed tester. A four-poster. Somehow she'd known Emma's aunt would have slept in one.

By the time she had eaten, and finished the coffee, the light outside was fading. She found four cut-glass candle sticks and put them to use. Then she set more candles around the room and lit some joss sticks. Tendrils of blue-grey, perfumed smoke snaked towards the plaster ceiling.

As she undressed, pulling off her studded boots, leather trousers and black T-shirt, she looked at her reflection in the large overmantel mirror. Her eyes looked huge in her narrow face. Candlelight flickered on her pale skin, the garish Medusa mass of her hair.She stood naked except for a fishnet body, admiring the slender curves of her waist, the flow of her hips. Behind her the bedroom had an odd look, somehow vibrant, larger than life. It was she who looked two-

51

dimensional, like a cardboard cut-out against the Victorian clutter.

It seemed that the house looked at her. Rose let it look. Stroking her hands over her breasts, she moved them downwards over the slight pout of her belly. She caressed the rose tattoo on her left hip, dipped her fingers between her thighs and stroked the dark hair that poked through the fishnet.

This house was a real turn-on. She had fantasised about it for months, ever since Emma showed her the place where the reclusive old girl had lived. She couldn't believe that the house would be Emma's one day. That night she had dreamed about living there. The obsession to spend one night alone in the house had begun soon after. The dare was just an excuse, a vehicle for her to have her own way. One night. That was all it would take.

'I'll make you mine,' she said to the shadows. 'Mine and Emma's.'

In the morning she'd bring Emma up to this room, persuade her with lips and tongue and deft slippery fingers that they should move in. They would lie on this bed together and make love in the dusty gloom. She would show her lover that there was nothing to fear. But first . . .

Slowly now. She breathed in the vanilla scent of incense. Light sparked on the jewel in her nose as she lifted her arms and untied the rags from her hair so that it spilled over her shoulders in a tangle of vibrant red. Shivering slightly with anticipation, she climbed onto the bed.

The dusty velvet coverlet was prickly against her skin. She closed her eyes. The house seemed to settle around her, the shadows moving in closer. A knot of excitement gathered in her stomach. Again she imagined lying on the bed with Emma. Her hands moved over her body in a slow dance. She spent a long time stroking her breasts, cupping the underswell, lifting and squeezing the firm flesh. She loved touching her breasts. The nipples were darkly defined and incredibly sensitive. When she was fully aroused they stuck out in wanton little tubes. Sometimes she came when Emma did nothing but suckle them.

Her breath came faster as she unfastened the fishnet body at the crotch, drew it up to her waist and tucked it tightly beneath her. The constriction around her waist, the nakedness of her hips and legs, excited her further. The fishnet made little indentations in the flesh of her breasts, quilting her. Her nippes were hard little nubs, bisected by thin black threads. The tactile feel of the cords made her shiver with lust.

Slowly, so slowly, she made circles on her bare lower stomach, working down to the patch of damp, scented hair between her thighs. Raising her knees, she let them fall apart and felt the caress of the dusty air on her parted sex. She sighed, the sound rustling into the room to be absorbed by the draperies. With the fingers of one hand, she pressed open her labia, exerting a slight pressure upwards so that her clitoris stood proud of the surrounding flesh.

Rose screwed her eyes shut, concentrating on the overall feeling of sensuality, of the cloying presence of the house all around her, and on the tension building, building between her thighs. She slid her hand downwards, dipped into the wet folds and touched the slippery moisture to the erect bud of her clit.

The whisper in her ear was subtle. The voice, soft and so husky with desire. Rose was startled, but somehow not afraid.

Her eyes snapped open. She searched the darkness, but could see nothing – no one. There was a new air of tension within the room. A faint smell of musk and lilies. Rose became aware of a presence. It was enticing. Amorphous. Something within her leapt to meet it.

The darkness was grainy, empty – gilded in small pools by candlelight and the thin shafts of moonlight that penetrated the stained-glass windows. Rose smiled, feeling disappointed. Wishful thinking. Too many vampire novels. Anne Rice and Freda Warrington had a lot to answer for.

Then the shadows moved.

The breath caught in Rose's throat. Her mouth went dry with anticipation even while a heady pulse ticked between her legs.

'Come then,' she said softly.

And the darkness changed. A faint glow appeared at its centre, thickened and took on form. A woman stood at the side of the bed. She was naked, dark-haired, pale and beautiful. Moonlight threw speckled shadows over her translucent flesh. Jewel colours against the white. The whisper came *inside* Rose's head. It was sibilant, insistent.

'Please. Let me. I beg you.'

Rose felt incapable of movement. Crazy images flooded her mind. This had to be a dream. An hysterical laugh bubbled up from deep inside her. But I'm awake. This is real. Her hands had fallen to her sides, the palms cupped as if in submission or supplication. Between her open legs, her exposed sex was beating like a second heart.

Then the woman bent over and kissed her. Her touch was cool, gentle at first. She climbed onto the bed and lay beside Rose; so light – she seemed weightless. Rose's thighs trembled as long white fingers played over her skin. Scented breath brushed her cheek, a wet tongue entered her ear. The arms encircling her were slender, pale, but very strong. Rose felt herself drawn into the woman's cold embrace. Full breasts pressed softly against her own. The woman moaned softly, beginning to move from side to side so that the tips of her big, firm nipples brushed backwards and forwards across Rose's own.

Rose felt slivers of pleasure flood her belly. She arched to meet the woman, making little sounds of urgency deep in her throat. The woman's skin grew warmer. It felt silky soft where it met Rose's naked flesh. The bunched-up fishnet was a barrier between them, but that fact excited Rose almost unbearably. The combination of skin to skin, the scratchy tightness around her waist and breasts, the dusty air on her lower limbs were all mesmerising.

Rose bent her head and closed her lips around a nipple. It was firm, rubbery. Drawing it deeply into her mouth, she lashed it with her tongue. She squeezed the breast hard, so that it was offered up to her, and released the nipple for a moment. Curving her tongue, she lapped at the taut bud, which was shiny, polished with her saliva. Then Rose felt herself pressed gently backwards, her arms held above her head.

Rose turned her face into the flesh of her own upper arm as long insistent white fingers began stroking her thighs. Pointed finger-nails played over her pubis and scratched gently up and down the sides of her swollen labia. Rose groaned aloud, biting into her own arm. She wanted the torment to end – she wanted it to go on . . .

Long black hair brushed her thighs and lay like a silk scarf across her stomach. Rose parted her legs, pushing upwards with her hips and arching her back. Long spiked fingers opened her sex, then Rose felt the first delicious sweep of a tongue on her wet inner lips. Her stomach grew taut, her hips worked back and forth as the hot tongue flicked upwards, feathering against the little flesh-hood covering her clitoris. The sweet, pulsing ache gathered momentum.

When Rose thought her pleasure would surely spill over, the contact was broken abruptly.

Before she could protest she found herself flipped over onto her stomach, her face pressed to the dusty velvet bedcover. Long claws dragged her buttocks apart and the hot lapping resumed. This time it started at the pouch of her sex, progressed up her cleft and over the tight pink ring of her anus. Rose cried out, her thighs rigid with tension, her wide-spread buttocks jerking and trembling as a firm tongue-tip entered her.

Somehow she held back as the knowing fingers dug into her flesh, holding her open and exposed. The velvet coverlet pricked her belly. Vanilla smoke tickled her nostrils. Now and then she felt long finger-nails scratching gently at her anus, probing into her soaking sex. When two fingers entered her, lifting gently, pulling in a backwards motion then slipping in and out, the first shudders broke over her.

In the very midst of her orgasm, she felt the bite of pain as sharp teeth scored her buttocks, long nails raked her back. Rose's cries echoed round the room, seemed to reflect back at her from the stained-glass window. The pleasure was so singular, so acute, that for a few moments darkness descended.

When she opened her eyes, she was lying with

her head hanging over the side of the bed. Her whole body seemed possessed by a tingling ache, as if it were reliving the experience at a new and deeper level. Rose lifted her head. The pale figure of the woman was standing a distance away, looking down at her. On her lovely face was an expression of pleading. It seemed to Rose that the figure was fainter. The line around her shoulders was smudged, half-absorbed into the darkness.

The whisper came again, hot inside Rose's head, but more hesitant this time.

'Only stay. And I'll come often to pleasure you. I exist only for you. I am what you make me. Please give me a reason to remain . . .'

The hand that reached out to Rose was almost transparent. The darkness crowded in, beginning to engulf the fading glow of the woman's body. Rose smiled joyfully. No wonder Emma's dotty old aunt had never left the house. What delights she had found within the sturdy walls.

She knew exactly what she must do.

Reaching out, she took hold of the fading swell of the woman's hips and pulled her close. As she wrapped her arms around the pale thighs, she felt them filling out and growing solid under her fingers. She pressed her face to the soft belly, her cheek against the curling hair that grew in a perfect triangle shape. As she breathed in the pungent scent of musk and lilies, she felt an instant reawakening of desire.

Bending her head, she parted the sex-lips with

58

her tongue, took her first taste of the rich salty flesh. The cold skin warmed again under her fingers. The hands that gripped her shoulders as she quested deeper were once again strong, the nails sharp, beautifully cruel. As Rose pulled the woman back onto the bed and pressed her thighs apart, she thought briefly of Emma who would be calling for her in a few hours. Emma who needed persuading.

A sense of certainty settled over Rose. The house was hers already. One night was all Emma would need.

Therapy

'SO, WHAT DO you do to combat executive stress? I love to go shopping myself. Nothing like a new outfit to give me a lift.'

The nasal voice of Linda the fashion editor floated into Anna's office as she sat staring at the screen of her Apple Mac battling with a feature which would not come right. She pushed back her chair in frustration and began paying attention to the conversation outside.

'I play squash. Sometimes treat myself to a facial or a leg wax.'

That was Corrina, deputy fashion editor. Both women in the corridor had recently joined the editing team of 'Pzazz' magazine, gaining the coveted jobs by calling in favours from high-ups in the trade.

Squash? A leg wax? Shopping? God help us! Anna thought. Is that the best they can come up with to fill their spare time? She had an impulse, quickly squashed, to go and tell them what she had planned for relaxation later in the day. How their perfectly made-up faces would go blank with disbelief.

Cheered by the thought, Anna opened her desk drawer and took out an envelope. Inside was the letter she had received that morning, along with three black and white photographs. Picking up the phone, she pressed the button for an outside line and dialled.

'Oh, hello. Anna Siegal here. Number two seems eminently suitable for my purposes. No problem with availability? Good. Look forward to our meeting.'

She replaced the receiver, a secret smile playing around her lips. Glancing at her wrist-watch she saw that she had two hours to go before she had to leave the office for the afternoon appointment. She poured herself a cup of black coffee, then turned her attention back to her Mac. Moving the mouse, she clicked on 'edit'. She'd have this feature finished before she left if it killed her.

Later, on her way to the lift, she passed Corrina, her arms full of an assortment of garishly coloured silk scarves.

'Accessories for the piece on Hermès,' Corrina explained. 'Off to the therapy centre for your regular session, are you? You never did say why you go there. What is it, some sort of Weight Watchers?'

'Not exactly,' Anna said breezily. 'It's more a whole body experience. Does wonders for one's well-being. Crouching over a desk all day is so draining.'

'Doesn't help the cellulite either, darling,' said Corrina, glancing meaningfully at Anna's bulging black leggings.

Skinny-arsed cow, Anna fumed, watching Corrina's stick-thin body diminish down the corridor. But despite her silent protestations, the pointed remark had hit home. As Anna drove across London to the treatment centre, she pondered on all the years she'd spent working on her insecurities. Today she prided herself on her ability to love her big, curvaceous frame. It was galling that, with a few words, Corrina had managed to transport her back to the days of her lumpy, spotty and painful adolescence.

Boy, did she need today's session! The therapy was an amazing confidence booster, leaving her feeling secure in the knowledge that it was downright sexy to be a generous size eighteen. On reaching Hampstead, she parked her car in a side street, then entered the door of the discreet clinic. The building was a restored Georgian town house. There was nothing in the black, wrought-iron railings or the window-boxes bursting with red geraniums and blue lobelia to suggest the nature of the therapies on offer.

Anna paused at Reception. The pleasant-faced woman behind the stained ash desk smiled at her.

'Ah, Ms Siegal. Nice to see you again. You are expected. Do go on up to treatment room three. Your therapist will be with you shortly.'

Anna thanked the woman and went up the stairs. The interior of the clinic was all marble columns, black tiles and white paintwork. On the second floor, she opened the door marked number three and went inside. The room was sparsely furnished. There were white Venetian blinds, a screen, a chair, a metal table with a lamp, and a leather-covered treatment table.

Anna slipped behind the screen and began to undress. There was a white cotton gown hanging up ready for her use. When she was naked, she put it on. It had ties at the front, unlike those hospital gowns that allowed your bottom to protrude rudely. As she emerged from behind the screen the door opened and a young man came in carrying a deep, covered tray. He was even more good-looking than in the photo. His shiny, dark hair was shoulder-length. It looked striking against his plain white regulation T-shirt and track pants.

'Good afternoon, madam,' he said. 'My name's James. I'm your chosen therapist for today.'

Anna smiled approvingly. His demeanour was perfect – friendly but courteous. Clients at the clinic were never addressed by name. Anna liked the anonymity, coupled with the knowledge that her express instructions would be carried out to the letter.

'Hello, James,' she said. 'I feel rather tense today. I'm very much in need of your specialist services.'

He smiled, showing even, white teeth. He was really sexy with his straight nose, olive-toned skin, and liquid brown eyes. Under the tight-fitting T-shirt, she could see the outline of toned pectorals and a flat, hard stomach. At the thought of his hands on her, her throat dried.

'I'm sorry to hear that you're stressed, madame. If you'd like to get up onto the treatment couch, I'll soon have you feeling better,' he said.

Anna made herself comfortable while James put the covered tray of instruments on the side table. He glanced swiftly at a computer print-out of her case notes, then said, 'No problem with your requirements. Ready to begin, madam?'

She nodded, feeling the usual mixture of anticipation. Each time she came to the centre her experience was slightly different. Her chosen therapist always found an individual way of meeting her particular demands.

'Let's just get you into the required position,' James said.

Anna trembled slightly as he untied the cotton robe and tucked the open flaps beneath her. Her pillowy breasts and big, round stomach were revealed. This moment always made her blush. It did not matter that she was totally in charge. Being naked before a handsome, desirable young man made her unbearably self-conscious. But she revelled in the flush of shame. That was part of the treatment. And there were worse indignities to come.

'May I say that madam has lovely breasts,' James said, looking her over appreciatively. 'They're big but firm. And your nipples are gorgeous. Prominent and such a pretty shade of pink. Your lovers must adore sucking them.'

He sounded sincere. She could almost believe that he had not been prompted by the explicit instructions on her record card. She sighed as he ran gentle fingers over her belly and soft, rounded thighs, before lifting each leg in turn and placing her feet in obstetric stirrups. She felt the cool air of the room between her thighs as they were drawn widely apart. Her face was bright red now. She did not meet his gaze as he slipped padded straps around the tops of her thighs, seating them high up under the swelling of her buttocks before securing them to posts at the side.

Anna began to feel excited. This handsome young man had an unobstructed view of her open sex. The urge to try and draw her legs together was almost overwhelming.

'Madam has a very generous figure,' James said, trailing his fingers over her skin. 'What a lovely soft belly. Such strong white thighs. And, if I may comment, a firm and well-made vulva. The labia are pink and nicely plump. It would be even better if you were depilated. I'll see to that for you at once.'

'Oh, do you think so?' Anna said, her pulses clamouring at the thought of him shaving her. 'Well, if you're sure . . .'

She loved this slow lead-up, the well-chosen comments, designed to make her feel like the most desirable woman in the world. James made certain that she was comfortable, positioning her so that her bottom was almost at the edge of the table. Then he adjusted the leather-covered rest behind her head and shoulders, so that from the waist up her body was slightly raised.

'I'm sure you'd like to see what I'm doing, madam,' he said. Lastly he placed her wrists above her head and secured them with bandages to the rail provided.

Deliciously helpless now, Anna watched James uncover the tray on the side table. She heard the snapping sound as he pulled on disposable rubber gloves. She shivered, awaiting the first touch, as he assembled the things he needed. Placing a chair between her legs he used an old-fashioned brush to apply a thick layer of shaving soap. The feathery bristles were a sweet torture as they flicked against her stretched labia and hardening clitoris.

Anna held her breath as he shaved her with long, expert strokes of a cut-throat razor. It was thrilling to feel the sharp metal skimming so close to her intimate membranes. All too soon it was over. James sluiced her pudenda with warm water and dried her.

'That's better,' he said. 'I can see your lovely stiff little clit more clearly now. It's standing proud of the surrounding labia as if greedy for attention. Naughty thing! It'll have to wait. Ready for the next stage?'

Anna did not trust herself to answer as he squeezed a large blob of transparent lubricant into the palm of one hand. She held her breath, anticipating the coolness of the gel on her hairless quim. But he did not go directly to stand between her spread thighs. Swooping down he pressed his mouth to hers.

The kiss was as prolonged as it was unexpected. A deep, sensual exploration. His tongue invaded her mouth, seeking, tasting. When he drew away she felt subtle tendrils of desire worming their way into her belly. She gave a muffled groan, no longer able to hold back the evidence of her pleasure.

'I think madam is ready now,' James said, satisfied that he had shattered her composure.

When he spread the lubricant on the folds of her sex, she gasped at the cold, oily feel of it. He stroked her gently, pulling at the labia until they swelled and stood out thickly. While he massaged her engorged sex-lips, he inserted two gloved fingers of his other hand and anointed her vagina with another generous blob of lubricant. She felt it dripping out of her, running warmly down the crease of her bottom.

It was difficult to stay still. She wanted to arch

her back, exert a pressure on the stirrups, flex her calf muscles and strain against the supporting straps which held her buttocks apart, but she controlled herself somehow. There was more to come, much more. She didn't want to peak too soon.

'How does that feel, madam?' James asked, rubbing her belly with one palm while continuing to stroke her exposed pudenda with a feather-light touch.

'Very good. So far,' Anna said with mock brusqueness. Lord, that was a gross under-statement! It felt bloody wonderful. It would be worth coming to the clinic for this alone.

James's forehead creased. 'Only . . . good? Then I've been sadly remiss. I'm sorry if madam is displeased. Let me hasten to put things right.'

Anna let out her breath on a sigh. James was playing the game for all he was worth. He bent over the tray and then took up his position between her thighs again. She felt his deft hands on her sex, two fingers gently holding her labia open while he inserted a small, slender phallus into her vagina. Anna chewed at her bottom lip as he moved the phallus back and forth.

'How's that? Does it suit madam?'

'No,' Anna said. 'It's too small. But keep it aside. You can use it up my bottom later.'

James withdrew the phallus. 'Very well. How about this one?' he said, inserting a slightly larger rubber cock.

Anna pretended to consider. It was hard to concentrate with James's hands on her lubricated sex and the dildo buried deeply inside her. 'It's . . . um, not right yet,' she said.

James looked crestfallen. Then his face brightened as he held up a large, bright-red rubber cock. Anna shook her head. 'That's far too big,' she said, her mouth curving with feigned distaste. The dildo was truly obscene. A shiny red monster with thick veins twisting down the shaft and a bulbous, flared glans. The thought of having it inside her both horrified and fascinated her.

James began to reassure her, as she knew he would. 'I'm sure you'll find it fits perfectly, madam. Do try it. I'll go very slowly and use lots of lubricant.'

'I said no!' Anna snapped with mock rage, beginning to struggle against the wrist-bonds as James brought the cock close to her vulva. 'No! Stop it! Do you hear me!' Oh, God, don't stop, she pleaded silently. Just the thought of the horrid thing squeezing into her tight channel almost made her come.

James was too well trained to be swayed by her outburst. His fingers reached for her labia again, pressing them open and exerting a slight pressure upwards. His gloved palm brushed against Anna's stiffly erect clitoris as he placed the cock's blunt glans at her entrance.

'James, I order you not to push that vile thing into me! Oh, you wretch. Take it out. It's stretching me horribly. Oh, it won't go in. I know it won't.' Her thighs trembled as the thick shaft slipped partway into her. Christ, it felt good.

James took hold of her oiled clitoris between his fingertips and pulled it gently back and forth. None of her other therapists had done this. He was using the nub of flesh like a tiny cock, masturbating it with measured efficiency.

'Oh, don't. You'll make me come too soon,' she moaned as the subtle drawing out of his fingers sent a spiked warmth flooding through her.

She felt herself loosening, opening up inside, accepting the impossibly big cock with ease. Lifting her head she peered between her thighs. The end of the cock was sticking rudely out of her. It dripped with lubricant and her own juices. The leather couch was awash beneath her buttocks.

She felt herself straining for release. Her orgasm was within reach. Then abruptly the stimulation was withdrawn. She almost wept with frustration. James chuckled. 'My, but you're wet, madam. I think we need the rubber sheet for the next stage.'

Anna let her head fall back against the leather rest as James lifted her bottom and smoothed the sheet beneath her. She ached to be penetrated again. It seemed that she was stretched from the intrusion of the thick red shaft. From the waist down she was a pulsing, throbbing mass of nerve-ends. James needed only to stroke her clitoris once or twice and she would climax.

He was approaching now, holding a rubber

70

douche-bag, a length of tubing, and a jug of warm water. Anna tensed, her ankles flexing in their supports. Oh, no. Not that. Even while she yearned for what was to happen, she dreaded the act itself. It was so shaming, so messy, and so . . . noisy.

'Please . . .' she said. 'I don't want . . .'

'Don't worry, madam,' James said soothingly. 'Almost finished now.' Swiftly he filled the douche-bag, attached the tubing, and hung the bag from one of the stirrups. There was a valve, operated by a cord which prevented the flow of liquid.

Carefully James inserted one end of the tubing into Anna's vagina. She made a sound of protest. But he smiled at the half-hearted gesture of defiance, knowing that pretending to be unwilling added immensely to her pleasure.

He held up the smallest of the dildos. 'Did you think I'd forgotten?' he said as he pushed it into her anus.

Anna closed her eyes as the slender stem filled her rectum. Filled front and back, she felt swamped by sensation. Penetrated by the tube of the douche-bag, her vagina was pulsing hungrily. Her anus convulsed around the slender dildo as if it would push it out. Then James did something else that none of her other therapists had done. He began to unzip his trousers. Taking out his cock he said, 'Look how hard you've made me, madam. I think you'd better do something about this.'

71

Oh, yes. Oh, God. Yes, she thought as he positioned himself beside her. His thick cock was near her face. The end of it was moist, the skin retracted to show the glistening purple glans. She smelt the salt-musk of his arousal and leaned across eagerly to take him into her mouth. As she began to suck, he groaned. A sound that seemed dredged up from somewhere deep inside him.

Anna shuddered, arching her back and straining against the constraints that made her subject to the delights of forced pleasure. As she pressed her buttocks to the table, the dildo was forced more deeply inside her anus. The tube of the douche-bag in her vagina was too small for her to gain purchase on. She bounced up and down, longing for the caress that would tip her over the edge.

'Oh, madam!' James said, his face screwed into an expression of bliss as she milked his rigid tool. Even as he started to come, he had the presence of mind to pull on the cord attached to the douche-bag.

As Anna felt his cock vibrate with the release of his sperm, a welcome surge of warm water entered her vagina. She swallowed James's salty come, a muffled scream rising to meet the flow as it slipped down her throat. As she climaxed the warm water poured out of her, spilling over the dildo in her stretched anus and splashing noisily onto the rubber sheet.

The sound of it, which seemed to Anna to be

the vocal expression of her forbidden pleasure, urged her on to experience a shattering, mind-blowing orgasm. The final paroxysms of pleasure were accompanied by the steady drip, drip, drip of water onto the floor.

James, having put his clothes to rights, went to stand between her thighs. He stroked and pinched her clitoris, making sure that she experienced two more climaxes before he deemed her satisfied. Anna's generous frame quivered and ripples ran over her fleshy belly as she orgasmed. The solid feel of her body as it gave itself to pleasure made Anna feel centred and at peace with herself. She felt that she'd truly died and gone to Heaven.

When the final pulsings had died away and she lay recovering, James said, 'Was the therapy to your liking on this occasion, madam?'

'Oh, yes. God, yes,' she breathed.

James beamed at her, his handsome face suffused with pride. 'It was a pleasure to service such a beautiful woman. Perhaps you'll choose me again?' And, even though there was no longer any need for him to humour his client, there was sincerity in his voice.

Anna basked in the warmth of James's regard. The glow of repletion lasted long after she left the centre and returned to her car. Later, when she returned to her office at 'Pzazz' she encountered Corrina in the cloakroom. 'Hi,' she said, giving the deputy fashion editor a dazzling smile. 'Busy afternoon?'

Corrina took one look at Anna's glowing face and her mouth fidgeted. 'Looks like your therapist did you the world of good,' she said grudgingly. 'Perhaps you should recommend her to me.'

'Him, actually,' Anna said. 'Recommend to you? Oh, I doubt whether you'd benefit. Only fatties like me need these sessions.'

'Yes, I suppose you're right,' Corrina said with mock sympathy. 'Well, you keep going to that centre. All it needs is will-power and you could be as slim as me.'

As Corrina turned away, looking smug, Anna smiled serenely. She felt no need to make a parting comment. No need at all.

The Music Lesson

AS I MOUNT the stairs the feeling begins, low in the pit of my stomach, a mixture of dread and anticipation.

The porter carries my cello case into the room and places it by the window. I tell him to collect me in one hour. The room is empty – more than empty: bereft without you in it. I walk across it, my buttoned boots clicking on the bleached oak boards, and sit on the window seat, waiting.

The afternoon light streams in through billowing muslin curtains. Outside in the street a breeze rustles the leaves of the plane trees. I stare at the buildings opposite, their wrought-iron balconies crowded with tubs of flowers – lilies, mimosa, roses. The white stucco is dazzling in the summer light.

When the door to the studio opens, I do not look around immediately, wanting to suspend the moment until I see your face. When I turn, I see that you are not very remarkable. I know how you must seem to others, but you are large in my thoughts. Hair of mid-brown, a longish serious face, your fine eyes obscured by gold-rimmed spectacles.

But it is your mouth that drives me mad and haunts my dreams. It is wide, finely sculpted. A music teacher should not have such a mouth. It is the thing which betrays your nature. Can others see that too? I saw it at once.

You smile and greet me – casual meaningless words. I cross to the other window and open my cello case. Nothing unusual in that. No one watching would think anything is amiss. But I know better.

We are to play together today, a Puccini duet. Seated, I position myself. One hand poised on the strings, the bow in my other hand. You sit opposite, aware of my every breath, but holding back your eagerness to touch me. I understand that perfectly. Anticipation is its own reward.

Three times you tap with your bow. A staccato of wood on wood that echoes the racing of my pulse. We begin. The music swells, fills the room, concentrating my senses. How beautiful, how stark is the sound in this room. The vaulted ceiling provides perfect acoustics.

My breathing is shallow and I am aware of the tightness of my corset. I drew the laces more tightly than usual. You love my tiny waist. Are you thinking of it now? Aching to encircle it with those slim, artistic hands? Or are you transfixed by the tops of my breasts where they bulge above the frosted lace of my chemise?

We play and I feel wholly alive.

I close my eyes and let the music sink into my blood and bones. I am quite taken over by it; it is breath and life and sensuality. We pause, smile at each other – conspirators. And play again. This time it is Verdi. I am growing warmer. The effort to play perfectly makes me tense. But that is not the only reason for my tension.

Then I am playing alone and it begins.

I dare not look at you as you lay your bow aside, lean your cello against the chair. This is too fragile to speak of, even to acknowledge. The music carries you to me and now you stand behind me. Before you touch me, I feel you. A slight difference in the air, perhaps your breath, tobacco-scented, on my neck.

Then a touch, a finger brushes my nape, just below the upsweep of my hair. I do not falter in my playing or give any sign that I have noticed your proximity. And you touch me again, twining one chestnut curl around your finger.

'You are playing well,' you say softly. I nod to acknowledge your approval – such a subtle gesture for something which means so much.

Another touch. This time your lips trace a path down my neck and pause at the slight bump of my spine, which is prominent when I bend my head to play. I shudder when I feel your tongue moving on that place – hot, tactile.

Your hair smells of hay and is silky when it brushes my bare shoulder. I wore this dress today because of its wide neckline and I'm glad that I did. There's the tiniest sound when your lips kiss my shoulder, almost lost in the music, little more than a sigh. But I hear it. Oh, I hear it.

Fingers on my buttons, undoing each peach-flushed pearl, one by one. I hold my breath when you part the fabric of my tight bodice and draw it back over my shoulders. I am wearing russet velvet today over a skirt of ashes-of-roses figured silk. I know these colours please you. They make the paleness of my skin seem opalescent and deepen my hazel eyes to lion-gold.

Your whisper is loud in my ears. Oh, you break the rules! Except for the music instruction we have always been silent, but I forgive you. I knew today would be special.

I play on, even though your fingers move over the tops of my breasts. I am trembling now. The bow screeches. It needs resin, but my need is greater.

Outside in the carriage my father waits for me. I am his pride, his possession. His head is cocked to listen to the music. If I were to falter he would clump slowly up the stairs, demand to know why we are wasting his money talking.

Today I am bold and turn my face towards you. I see that you are surprised. You think me innocent, unknowing, but I learn fast – a model pupil. Perhaps you disapprove, but you do not disappoint me. Our lips meet. How tender is your mouth – the mouth you should not own. You taste of brandy and cigars, and something else . . . indefinable. A young man's taste. You are like a symphony. Is that too trite? Certainly it's not original. I do not care.

Your fingers slip below my neckline, into the top of my chemise and close at once over my breast. Ah, this is punishment for my wantonness. You intend to shock me. I gasp, my hand falters and the cello complains, but she forgives me at once.

My lips open beneath yours and I revel in the texture of your tongue. So tender, I want to bite it, suck it, but I repress the urge as your other arm slips around my waist. I lean back against you, feeling your strength. Arching my back I move my hips a little and your fingers become busy at my breast, stroking, pinching. Sweet pleasures trickle over my skin like notes of music.

You whisper to me, 'I'll make you come this time.'

I am dizzy with shock. You have never been so bold, nor I so unrestrained. The hand at my waist moves down and you withdraw your other hand from my breast. I am lonely without it, but not for long. When you have lifted the layers of my skirts and found my thigh through the split in my cambric drawers you return.

Now I feel you on my naked flesh in two places at once. My breast seems to swell as it welcomes your return. The other hand is caressing my inner thigh, moving up slowly, trailing like silk on my skin and, even now, you find the moist red heat of me. I tense, afraid for a moment. I should not allow this, but it was inevitable. And was so from that first time in the lesson when you stopped playing and I carried on without question or pause.

'Oh,' I breathe, when your fingers begin to stroke me . . . there.

Such a little sound, but it echoes inside me and melds with the music. Would I love you if you could not play the cello? Probably not. 'Oh,' again as your fingers describe circles, pressing and smoothing, dipping between the widely spread folds to caress the small bump which is burning, throbbing.

Now I am lost in your kiss and I play by rote, my arm moving the bow with the expertise of long practice, of many painful lessons when my fingertips bled. My knuckles remember the punishment of a wooden ruler. My first teacher. Not you. A new rhythm is building, building inside me and I follow the cadence of your voice. Another symphony.

'Reach for it, my little Clara,' you say with your soft, European accent. I love the way you say my name.

How can I let go – make myself vulnerable to you? That is to give you too much power. Where can this lead? But I cannot stop. As I continue to play, you stroke me, your slender, beautiful musician's fingers playing out their matchless tune on my most intimate flesh.

It seems as if all of me is poised, waiting. Always waiting. I am lost in the magic of the moment. The sun streams in and makes bars of gold on the pale oak floor. I smell lavender polish and resin, the warm leather lining from my cello case by the window. Your breath, a fragrant benison.

I can hardly stop myself calling out. How exquisite it feels to have you touching me. And now entering me in two places with tongue and fingers. Though my flesh sheathes you I cannot move my lower body very much: the cello, my position, prevents it. So I must endure and trust you to lead me. And you do. Like the impresario you are, you lay the notes one on top of the other.

The piece is almost finished. I must reach a peak before I draw the bow across the strings for a final time. Can I do as you wish? You have been training me expertly and I do not want to fail. Oh, my cheeks are burning with shame and exertion and I feel you licking the slight sheen of sweat from my top lip. Your tongue so hot, questing. I almost beg you to stop.

Lord, I am strung as tight as my bow. But it is beginning now.

'Ah, yes, Clara, my angel. Let it go,' you whisper softly against my ear.

It is the final movement and I feel myself gather, break, convulse. How like music it is, sinews and membranes resonating to a top note which spreads and flows over me, enervating, enriching. You capture my groans in your mouth, taking the sounds deep into the warm cavern of your throat.

And I give them to you, my music master. A most singular duet, don't you think?

Your fingers are deft as they pull up my bodice and fasten the pearl buttons. When you take your seat you smile, just for an instant. Behind your spectacles your fine dark eyes are filled with pride. What an obedient pupil I am. Picking up your bow, you tap out the notes. Wood on wood, staccato, echoing the rhythm of my racing pulse. You join me in a duet. Faultless, never a note wrong.

And the last moments meld together, until – silence.

In the carriage outside, Father is nodding his head with satisfaction. His money has not been wasted, neither have I wasted a precious moment by stopping to talk. My playing is improving immensely. Soon I'll be ready for another teacher, he says.

But for now I shall continue to come here once a week. I stand, shake out my crumpled skirts, and put my beloved cello inside its case. The porter is at the door now, waiting. He picks up my cello and I follow him to the top of the staircase.

'Well done, Clara,' says my teacher, softly. 'You are almost ready.'

I do not look back. Downstairs father is waiting impatiently.

The Huntress

AS THE SMALL chartered plane began losing altitude, curving around in a graceful arc, Ruth Shepard leaned forward in her executive-class seat. Through breaks in the clouds she could see the ocean far below, a vast gleaming expanse of aquamarine.

Ruth smoothed the skirt of her designer suit then glanced at the woman who sat next to her, an eye-mask covering the upper part of her face. Nancy Brogan, a high-up in a prestigious American design company, was snoring softly. She had been asleep since their conversation at the start of the journey. Ruth wished she was calm enough to doze, but her mind kept dwelling on what Nancy had said. When Ruth asked her if she had received a letter, Nancy had replied, 'Sure. Mine came in the mail at my company office. I expect this is going to be another of those hare-brained schemes to hone my management skills. You would not believe the seminars and courses I've attended.' She rolled her eyes and shrugged. 'I just do as I'm told. He-who-must-be-obeyed holds the corporate purse-strings!' She opened a Gucci handbag and unfolded a single sheet of paper. 'This is the letter. I guess every woman on this plane has one similar.'

Ruth had glanced at the letter. It was exactly the same as the one she had received. Nancy had been told to pack and go to the airport. All travel arrangements were taken care of. She could expect to be away for a minimum of five days. There was no question of choice. The letter was a demand.

'If you're here, then I guess someone pulls your strings too, huh?' Nancy said, when Ruth handed the letter back.

Ruth nodded. 'Behind every successful woman . . .'

'There's another successful woman or man, waiting to push you aside and claw their way to your desk!' Nancy chuckled.

'Exactly.' Ruth laughed with her. 'That's why I've accepted this challenge. No questions asked. I'll do whatever I need to to give me an edge over the competition.'

'Smart lady.' Nancy grinned. 'These high-powered aptitude tests are the fashion right now. Who knows what'll be flavour of the month next?'

Ruth thought it was more likely that they were

all being head-hunted by a multi-national company. If that was the case, then she was part of a most exclusive short-list. Everyone on the plane was an expert in their chosen profession.

'We're about to land,' Ruth said now, peering intently at the thickly forested hills.

Nancy sat up, took off the eye-mask, and stretched. 'Where the hell are we? Oh, God is that the runway? It looks like a goat track! Better hold on tight, ladies!'

As Ruth stepped out of the plane, the heat pressed against her face like a hot, wet blanket. Within seconds she was dripping, her expensive haircut drooping and clinging to her skull. She felt a surge of irritation. The last thing she wanted was to arrive looking sticky and dishevelled. She hoped there would be time to freshen up before the welcome meeting. Ruth always travelled with a barrage of cosmetics and toiletries.

It was a relief to step into the relative coolness of one of the waiting vehicles. Twenty minutes later the four-by-four drew up in front of an Hawaiian-style village of bamboo walled apartments, complete with palm-thatched roofs and a pool-side bar. Bowling-green-quality lawns surrounded the bungalows. Brightly coloured tropical flowers were everywhere. Men dressed in spotless white uniforms came to welcome the women and show them to their rooms.

'Please to come this way, ma'am,' a young man said to Ruth.

'See ya later, alligator,' Nancy called.

Ruth's room was small, but charming. A basket of fruit stood on a bamboo table. Next to it was a welcoming card. She was instructed politely to change into suitable clothes, then to meet for further instructions in the building she could see from her window. She unpacked shorts, a white cotton shirt and a pair of sandals before taking a shower. After dressing and finger-drying her thick brown hair, she applied fresh make-up. It was cool in her room, due to the air-conditioning. She did not relish stepping out into the fierce tropical heat again.

Ruth was a city girl, born and bred. She liked order and neatness in her life. The sprawling lushness of the vegetation, just feet away from her bungalow, made her feel uneasy. Well, there was no help for it. She needed to know what was going on. Hastily plaiting her damp hair, she left it hanging over one shoulder. As she left her bungalow, she saw another of the women leaving her apartment. She recognised Sarah Reynolds. Sarah worked for a firm of London bankers. The two women fell into step.

'Have you any idea what to expect?' Sarah said. She was slightly built and had curly dark hair caught up high on her head with a towelling band. She looked enviably cool in a white halter top and tailored shorts. Her slender legs were shown to advantage by strappy high heels.

'None at all,' Ruth said, wishing that she'd

worn prettier sandals instead of settling for comfort over style. 'But I've a feeling all is about to be revealed.'

Ruth and Sarah entered the meeting place together. The other women, except for Nancy, were already there. They sat on woven grass mats which covered the beaten earth floor. How incongruous we all look squatting here in our designer shorts, our perfect make-up already starting to melt, Ruth thought.

'Hiya, gals,' Nancy said, breezing in through the door. 'Oh, am I last? Story of my life!' There was a polite ripple of laughter. Nancy looked stunning in an emerald green bathing suit, with a Hermès scarf tied sarong-style around her waist.

'Welcome, ladies,' said a deep male voice. 'May I have your attention?'

A tall man dressed in a white linen suit stepped from behind a bamboo screen which had been in half shadow at the back of the single room. Ruth's heart gave a lurch when she saw that sculpted, perfect facial structure framed by sun-streaked hair. She recognised this man. He was the owner of an airline company, amongst other things, and was known for his ruthless business dealings. He was also extremely eligible, wealthy, arrogant, and too attractive for his own good.

'I'm here to give you instructions,' Joel Matheson said. 'Make certain you listen closely. I cannot stress this enough. After you leave this room, you're on your own.' Matheson grinned narrowly. 'You'll be engaging in a contest – an ancient rite. This challenge is like nothing you've ever experienced. The islanders who used to live here had a name for the ceremony. The rite was enacted every mid-summer. The most beautiful women would be chosen to take part. Just like you've been chosen. Roughly translated the native word means 'Animal woman takes power from the Sun'. There'll be one winner. The woman who triumphs over the rest will receive my personal cheque.' The amount of money he spoke of was obscene.

Ruth tried not to let her surprise show on her face. The other women were staring at Matheson openly, one or two of them making it quite clear from their expressions that they would do *anything* to become the victor in this bizarre contest.

'So we have to compete against each other?' Nancy said, flicking back a lock of her blond hair. 'You've brought us all this way to tackle a native obstacle course?'

Matheson smiled slowly, his teeth very white in his tanned face. 'Oh, nothing so pedestrian. Give me credit for presenting you with a much more compelling challenge. You'll all need to get in touch with your base natures. In short, throw off the veneer of civilisation completely, return to a simpler, more savage time.'

When he finished speaking there was a stunned silence. Ruth was the first to speak. 'To what purpose? I mean – what's the goal?'

Matheson turned his dark blue gaze on her. For the first time she felt the full force of his persona. His charm was almost hypnotic. He grinned slowly. 'In the old times a male was chosen and the women would run him to ground and overpower him – sexually. Are you capable of abandoning yourselves entirely to your essential female natures, or are you constrained by what the world expects of you?'

Before their astonished gazes he undressed. Wearing only a brief leather garment around his waist, he stood up and faced them. Ruth felt the urge to giggle. Matheson was the quarry. Me Tarzan. You Jane. What an arrogant bastard. The prospect of running him to ground was ridiculous, but she could see that Matheson was utterly serious. And the amount of money he had dangled before them as a prize made this whole venture far more than the crack-pot game of a bored playboy.

'Everything you'll need is in the knapsacks behind the screen,' he went on. 'This island's covered in jungle. There's no wild animal large enough to harm you – if you're careful. There's plenty of water and food to be found. And you can't get lost. In two hours you can walk from shore to shore in any direction. My people here will keep tabs on you, but they won't make themselves known unless you need medical help. Are there any questions?'

'When do we start?' Sarah Reynolds said, her

face flushed and her dark eyes glittering with excitement. Drops of perspiration sparkled on her curly hair.

'The contest's already begun. Whatever you're wearing, that's it. There's no returning to the village. Anyone who wants to drop out can do so. But the plane won't return for three days.'

'And no doubt there'll be a less than complimentary letter to our company bosses if we refuse to take part,' Ruth said dryly.

'Very astute,' Matheson said, raking her with a measuring gaze.

Ruth was grateful now that she'd instinctively worn practical clothes. Sarah glanced down at her high-heeled fashion shoes in dismay. Matheson grinned nastily and Ruth felt a surge of dislike. He had deliberately refrained from forewarning any of them about what was to come in the hope that they'd put themselves at every disadvantage. But then, that too was part of the challenge.

She felt a heat in the base of her belly and knew that, despite herself, she was stimulated by the prospect of what was to come. Lifting her chin she looked straight at Matheson, trying to ignore the fact that he had the most perfect body of any man she had ever seen. Anyone else would have looked ridiculous with the scrap of leather around his waist, but he managed to look virile and poised.

It would have given him the greatest satisfaction to know that she was wondering what his skin felt like to the touch. The thought of besting him was exhilarating. That sculpted mouth was made for kissing . . .

'And when one of us catches you,' she said levelly. 'What happens then?'

Matheson's eyes sparked wickedly. '*If* any of you do. Use your imagination. The islanders had a saying: "When woman is queen, man must bow before her and offer himself for her pleasure." Conquer me and you become the victor. You'll know what to do. Take what you want from me. That is your right.'

And with that he disappeared out of the door. After Matheson had gone, there was consternation. Ruth did not bother to join in with the questioning. To her mind any more discussion was futile. She reached behind the screen and extricated a haversack. As she sat on the floor and began looking through the contents she found herself joined by Nancy and Sarah.

'Jeeze, I wish I'd put on shorts and a blouse,' Nancy said, plucking at her emerald swimming costume.

Ruth took out tubes of insect repellent and sun block and began to apply both. 'I doubt if we'll need to worry about clothes. It's hot enough to fry by day and I'll bet it's not much cooler by night.' At the door she glanced back. 'Good luck, everybody. See you in the jungle.'

Just a few yards from the village the jungle

pressed in, surrounding Ruth on all sides with a verdant ripe softness. There was a smell of heat, mildew, and something rich, like fruit cake. The humidity was incredible. Her shirt and shorts stuck to her wet skin. Rivulets of sweat trickled from under her hat band.

She used the knife she found in her pack to chop away at the vegetation on either side. But that was tiring, so she simply went slower, pushing aside the tough shiny leaves in her path. Her hair snagged on low branches and whippy stalks scratched her bare legs. When she backhanded her forehead, smears of greasy make-up came away. Oh, what the hell, she thought, who's going to care what I look like in this heat? Resolutely she ignored the inner voice which told her that this whole situation was ridiculous, that she had no more chance of tracking down Matheson than of flying to the moon.

. In her private and working life, Ruth refused to contemplate defeat. But the habit of self-control had become an obsession. In her career any sign of weakness was scented out by the bloodhound wannabes in the offices on the floor below hers. She'd had to be strong and ruthless to get ahead. But she denied, even to herself, that she had sacrificed something inherently female in doing so. Matheson had hit a nerve when he challenged her to abandon herself to her essential feminine energies. When did you last feel sexy? the secret inner voice said. When did you last allow yourself to want a man just for his body and not for what he could get for you in the company?

Her sandals were silent on the thick leaf mould underfoot. Insects whined and buzzed. She swore when she tore a nail on a rock, but somehow it did not seem very important. Back in London, a broken nail would have had her hurrying to a specialist salon to get it expertly wrapped. The heat pushed oily fingers under her skin. Runnels of perspiration trickled down inside her bra. The waistbands of her shorts and pants were soaked. Yet the discomforts seemed minor, compared to the beauty all around her.

Before long she found that she was walking with a loose open-hip sway, quite unlike her usual clipped stride. She could smell her body sweat and musk and gloried in the natural odours untainted by the false notes of manufactured perfume. Inside she felt as if she was melting, oozing out to meet the throbbing tropical heat.

A few yards on she came to a stream. It burbled and frothed over moss-covered rocks. With a cry of delight, she untied her sandals and slung them around her neck. Then she entered the water. The coolness around her ankles and calves was delicious. As she started downstream, making for the faint thunder of a waterfall, she felt herself uncoiling slowly, her body unravelling like a spring that was finally relieved of tension.

Apart from the cries of brightly coloured birds

and the shrieks of tiny gold monkeys, it was quiet in the dappled shade of tree ferns. Now and then she thought she glimpsed one of the other women, but no one answered when she called out. Then she caught herself, laughing. Fool, to call out to them! We're all in competition. All of us want the cheque that Matheson has promised.

The sunlight flashed on jade, emerald, scarlet, as tiny flies skittered around banana palms. Some of the bananas were ripe. Ruth cut some from the central stack. They were tiny and tasted creamy, not at all like supermarket fruit. She drank some water from the stream, then filled a canteen and slung the strap over one shoulder. Already it was growing dark. She hadn't thought about the time when she left the village. Now she realised that she must spend the night alone in the jungle.

She felt a dart of fear, then remembered that Matheson had assured them all that no wild animal on the island was big enough to harm them. Still, for precaution's sake, she looked for a safe place to sleep. She found a tree with huge twisted roots, beneath which was a small chamber. Crawling inside, she found it dry and clean. Curling up on the dry moss, Ruth blinked through the cage of roots.

One moment it was growing dark, then it was night. There was no twilight, just sudden moonlight when every leaf was silvered and the jungle sounds changed. The rhythm of the night sang in Ruth's blood. She felt a strange contentment. She knew that she must look a wreck, but she could not have cared less. Tree frogs croaked, plum-purple shadows gathered around her. Ruth stretched out her legs, pillowed her head on her arm, and slept.

It seemed that only a moment passed before a movement woke her. Something soft and hot was pressed to her stomach. A silken pressure moved up the inside of her thigh. Half asleep, Ruth stretched and allowed her head to fall to one side on the mossy pillow. This dream was so real. It was too delightful to break by opening her eyes, so she lay still, allowing the sensations to continue. The buttons of her blouse were being undone and her bra eased gently aside. Then she felt the sweetly pulling pleasure as her nipple was suckled. The hand on her thigh dipped under the hem of her shorts. Fingers moved over her underwear, stroking her pubis through the damp cotton. She was getting wet between her legs, her labia thickening, swelling. When a finger slid into her moist channel, she opened her legs and pressed down, wanting that subtle touch on her clitoris.

Suddenly Ruth was jerked awake. This was no dream! She sat up, her legs scrabbling on the moss, clawing backwards. In the darkness two eyes gleamed at her. She saw moonlight silvering a sculpted face, making hollows at cheeks and eye sockets. A man laughed huskily.

'Matheson! You bastard!' she hissed, ashamed

at her body's ready reaction to his caresses. 'What the hell are you playing at?'

He grinned, his teeth very white in the moonlight. 'I've been tracking you. It was almost too easy. Now I've come to claim my prize.'

'But I'm supposed to find you! You made no mention of taking some kind of forfeit if you should find one of us first.'

'Didn't I? I must have forgotten to mention it. But you didn't seem exactly unwilling just now.'

Ruth prickled with mortification. Despite his arrogance she could not deny that she wanted him. She could feel the wetness on her inner thighs. An insistent throbbing was spreading from her clitoris up into her lower belly. How was it possible to desire a man so much when you disliked him intensely?

'Oh, I get it now,' she said. 'This whole set-up is just for you. You get to seduce all of us in turn. We're the quarry! The rite you mentioned is a load of rubbish!'

'Oh, the rite existed as I explained and I intend to honour my promise – *if* one of you runs me to ground. But you see, I just don't think any of you are capable of doing so. The primal female energy no longer exists in the modern woman.'

'Don't be too sure of that,' Ruth said, drawing back as he bent over her.

His mouth came down to claim hers, his tongue pushing strongly into her mouth, tasting and possessing her. She meant to bring up her hands and push him away, but somehow she found herself clasping his shoulders. The voice of the jungle was loud in her head, the night heat acting like a spur to her senses. The hardness and warmth of Matheson's bare chest seemed to burn through her half-opened cotton blouse. Suddenly he was tearing at her clothes and she was helping him.

She had hardly time to wonder at herself, to marvel at the hunger raging through her, before she was wriggling out of her shorts. He used his thumbs to push down her pants, then he leaned into her. The column of his cock pressed against her inner thigh as she spread herself under him. As her body opened to his, she saw a mental image of an exotic flower with petals peeling back to reveal a moist centre, drenched with sweet nectar.

She made little moans of eagerness as the cock quested bluntly towards her, nudging past her parted labia and slipping deeply into her. He was hot and hard. Her flesh seemed to suck at him, drawing him in deeper, until the swollen head of the cock nudged against her womb.

'Oh, God . . .' Ruth lifted her legs and wrapped them around Matheson's lean hips. Raising her lower body she rubbed herself against him as he pounded into her, tipping up her hips so that he drove downwards into her red heat.

She had never felt anything like this. There was no finesse, no tenderness, nothing but a joint and urgent need. Their sweat-slick skin chafed and slid. She could not pretend, even to herself, that she did not crave the thrusting hardness, the sensation of being totally filled. Clawing at his taut buttocks, she surged back and forth, gasping with pleasure, her head thrown back in total abandonment. Something seemed to give way in her head. There was a sound in her ears, like throbbing drums. The jungle beckoned. Her clitoris mashed against his pubis and her climax built rapidly, rising to a crescendo that left her uttering guttural little cries as her body convulsed around Matheson's invading maleness.

A moment later he drew out of her and spilt himself onto her belly. Hardly pausing to catch his breath, he sat back on his haunches and reached for the scrap of leather.

'So you're something of a gentleman, despite evidence to the contrary,' Ruth said dryly, wiping her stomach with her shirt. Now that they had pulled apart, she found that she could not look him in the eye. Her cheeks burned. God, what had possessed her to act like a sex-starved cat on heat? She had not even thought of protection, until now. At least Matheson had had the grace to come outside her.

Matheson grinned wolfishly. 'I singled you out from the others. You're different, special. I'd like you, at least, to have a good opinion of me. Despite what you think, I do have a code of honour.' He began moving backwards out of her temporary shelter. 'Sleep well,' he said, before disappearing into the darkness.

Ruth slumped back on the carpet of dried leaves. If it had not been for the tingling and pulsing of her sex, the faint smell of semen and male sweat, she would have believed that she had just imagined the whole thing. *What is happening to me?* She did not recognise herself. Never had she given herself to anyone like that. And further more, she was still aroused. Tentatively she put her hand between her legs.

Her sex was hot and swollen, the labia puffed-up and her vagina awash with juices. She pushed a finger into herself, amazed at the muscular, fecund feel of her inner flesh. Almost without thought she slid another finger into her body and began rhythmically to push them both in and out. She began moving, weaving her hips back and forth, opening her legs wide. This was incredible. Why did she not feel guilty for touching herself? She always had before. That was why she rarely masturbated. Lowering her other hand, she tapped gently on her clitoris, feeling the way it swelled under her touch. Parting her fingers, she rubbed gently either side of the swollen bud. It felt so good. She panted audibly as she teased herself.

Rich, buttery juices coated her fingers. She drew them out to smear the slickness over her clitoris. A tension built inside her as she stroked and rubbed and stabbed at herself in an access of selfish pleasure. Her climax when it came was deep and satisfying, the sounds of her completion echoed in the moist tropical night, joining with the chorus of insects' chirrups. With her sweat cooling on her body, she snuggled naked into the dried leaves and slept.

The next morning Ruth crawled out from under the tree roots and looked around her. The jungle glittered in the sunlight. She breathed deeply of its loamy smell. The air was scented with vanilla and felt soft against her skin. Inside herself, she felt a further loosening as if some essential element had slid away during the night. Something was happening to her: the jungle had laid claim to her.

Deciding not to dress, she stuffed her clothes into her knapsack, then reached for the tube of sunscreen. Her hand halted in midair. Moved by an impulse beyond her control, she brushed aside the thick covering of leaves underfoot and scooped up handfuls of fragrant wet soil. Haltingly at first, she smeared the mud onto her skin, then began applying it with relish until her body was covered. The mud felt delicious. As it dried, some of it fell off in flakes, but most of it remained, affording protection from the sun's rays and providing her with natural camouflage.

Ruth's mouth curved in a smile as she thought of what had happened in the night. A new resolve had been born within her. She knew that she must find Matheson and prove him wrong. But how?

Setting off, she noticed a broken strand of a fern. In the soft earth there was the imprint of a bare foot. As she concentrated, she saw other, more subtle signs of Matheson's passing. With growing confidence she set out after him. As she walked, she came upon bushes bearing fruit and knew instinctively which to eat and which to leave alone. Picking a handful of berries she crammed them into her mouth. They were tart and chewy. The red juice streamed over her chin and dripped onto her breasts. Pausing only to rub the back of her hand over her mouth, she plunged more deeply into the undergrowth.

The sun was low, casting long shadows from the moss-covered rocks she passed. A purple-throated hummingbird whirred close, its tongue extended to probe the depths of a cream orchid. Ruth heard a faint sound and paused, scenting the air like a cat. Dipping low, she slid silently through the tangle of vines and ferns, emerging at the edge of a clearing. A pool sparkled in the near distance. On a flat, sun-warmed rock, a yard or so away, there were two figures.

Ruth sank into the dappled shade of a tree fern, obscuring herself from view. The two naked women had not heard her approach. They were engrossed in each other, oblivious to anything other than their own pleasure. Ruth's eyes widened as she took in the sight of Nancy Brogan and Sarah Reynolds kissing with animal passion. *Has the jungle changed them too*? She found herself transfixed by their languid movements, the way they strained against each other, pressing breast against breast.

When Nancy slid her hand between Sarah's thighs, Sarah moaned loudly and ground herself against her lover's fingers. Nancy whispered endearments, mouthing Sarah's shuddering skin as she stroked the curling hair on her mons. Ruth was so enthralled by the sight of the two women that it was a moment before she saw the figure in the bushes off to one side. Matheson. It had to be. And she knew that he had not detected her presence.

She felt a fierce excitement, knowing that this was the best chance she would have of surprising him. Stealthily she moved backwards and began circling around the clearing. As she grew near to where he was hiding, she lay on her stomach and began using her knees and elbows to propel herself forwards. Faintly she could hear Sarah's moans and Nancy's answering cries. Through the screen of vegetation she saw that Nancy was kneeling between Sarah's thighs, her head moving slowly back and forth as she tongued the other woman's vulva. Against the backdrop of the jungle, with the tropical sun beating down, the sight was somehow primeval, beautiful.

She smiled. Matheson was intent on spying on the lovers, waiting for them to finish before he revealed himself and claimed a forfeit. What a surprise *he* was going to get.

She could see him now. Only feet away, he was a shadowy form against the backdrop of an oleander. Silently, slowly, she edged forward and around the back of the bush. The two women's cries increased in tempo. She was close enough to hear Matheson's breathing and to know that he was aroused. She could actually smell his excitement, sense the pounding rhythm of his blood. Without pausing to contemplate just how she had become so super-sensitive, she slid through the long grass beside him and with a smooth, sinuous movement reared up before him.

Matheson's face went white. His mouth gaped. For a moment she thought he was going to have some kind of a seizure. A word escaped him. She had never heard it before, but she knew that it was the name of an ancient deity.

She nodded and held out her hand. 'I claim my right over you.'

Moving slowly, like a sleep-walker, Matheson fell to his knees. His face was filled with awe and longing. 'What . . . what do you require of me?' he stammered.

Ruth gestured, exulting in her power. Her breasts swelled and her nipples hardened, pushing against their coating of mud. She had forgotten how she must look, with her naked body caked with greyish powder, her thick brown

103

hair matted and tangled with leaves. But Matheson's expression reminded her. His handsome face was stricken by wonder. He had not believed the old stories, she realised, but he did now.

'On your back,' she ordered. 'Lie over that rock.'

Matheson did as he was bid. With his back curved over the rock, his head and arms hung back helplessly. Muscular parted thighs balanced his body weight. His body was curved into a bow, his erect cock sticking out potently. His scrotum was exposed, held in tight to his body. Ruth straddled him. Looking down at his white face, she felt herself grow gravid with power. The power of the jungle.

Slowly she bent her legs, sinking down towards the twitching column of flesh. Matheson groaned, suffused by fear and longing. Under the pressure of his erection, his foreskin had slid back to uncover the purplish glans. A glistening drop of pre-emission oozed out of the slitted cock-mouth. With the tip of one finger, Ruth scooped up the clear fluid and leaned forward to smear it across Matheson's sculpted mouth. He moaned, tremors passing over his skin as he circled his lips with his tongue.

Grasping the cock, Ruth swooped down to impale herself. As she sank down, enclosing the rigid flesh inside her hot and hungry vagina, Matheson gave a strangled scream and bucked against her. His hands clutched at air and he tossed his head from side to side. Ruth rode him mercilessly, lifting herself almost clear of his cock then slamming all the way down until her pubic hair ground against his.

She did not allow Matheson anything, but took her pleasure entirely for herself. Sweat snaked down her skin, making runnels in the dried mud. With her strong internal muscles, she milked him, forcing him to eject his semen in great shattering bursts while his chest heaved and he gasped, almost weeping in his ecstasy. Even then, she had no mercy. And Matheson did not expect any. He remained stiffly erect as she worked herself up and down on him, crying out in the acuteness of her pleasure while forcing him to spurt inside her again and again.

The feel of his hot organ as it pulsed against her flesh-walls, giving up its life-force at her command, drove her on to orgasm after orgasm. She was almost delirious in her sexual hunger and her domination over him. He was simply a male, an object for her pleasure.

When Matheson was sobbing unrestrainedly, trembling all over while in the throes of a final, merciless paroxysm, Ruth looked up to find herself observed. Sarah and Nancy were standing a few feet away, their arms linked fondly, expressions of wonder on their faces.

'Dear God. Ruth?' Nancy said, a slow smile coming over her face. 'Well, who'd have thought it!'

Ruth felt as if a haze was lifting from her brain. The jungle seemed to realign itself around her. Suddenly she was once again aware of the noises of insects, birds, and the gurgling of a spring that emptied into the pool ahead. She straightened slowly and felt Matheson's shrinking cock slip out of her. Silver runnels of semen slid down her thighs, but she ignored them, smiling at the women. Matheson struggled up from the rock. Throwing himself at her feet he pulled up handfuls of soft moss and began wiping her clean.

'I adore you,' he murmured. 'Adore you. No one's ever bested me. I've been waiting for you all my life.'

Nancy lifted an eyebrow. 'I'd say the cheque's yours. But somehow I can't see you being too bothered about business from now on. Do you know what you've taken on, honey?'

'I've never been clearer about anything in my life,' Ruth said, looking down at the man who knelt before her.

He was just as striking and arrogant, with his perfect face and his sun-streaked hair now dark with sweat. Anyone who knew him would see no change. But Ruth knew that there was something different about him. The acknowledgement of female power had changed him forever. And that was why she was certain about her destiny.

She knew now that she need no longer suppress any part of herself to get ahead in her professional life. What she had found in the jungle would never leave her entirely. Without a backward glance she walked towards the pool. Sitting in the shallow water, she began washing the mud from her body. A long shadow fell across her body.

'May I join you?' Matheson said, his voice uncertain and tinged with respect.

She smiled up at him. 'You may. And I think I should call you Joel from now on. Since we're intimately acquainted and likely to remain so.'

Wet Nurse

JEHANNE SAT BY the side of the road, waiting for the stage coach. It was almost noon and the sun beat down on top of her straw bonnet.

She was tired already, but there was still far to go. Her head drooped with dejection. She could do nothing but wait. At least the farmer had promised to meet her with his cart when she alighted at the coaching inn.

Jehanne knew that she ought to think herself lucky. Positions for wet nurses were getting fewer these days. Untying her pack, she took out the hunk of bread and piece of cheese she had saved for the journey. It did not take her long to finish eating. She opened the stopper on a leather bottle, but there was no water left. Sighing, Jehanne chewed on a stalk of grass. The green taste of it made her feel less thirsty.

It was another half hour before she felt the faint

vibration of iron-shod wheels on the road. The plume of dust was visible before the coach itself came into view. Wearily Jehanne pushed herself to her feet and picked up her pack. Gathering her long skirts around her, she climbed aboard. Her full breasts pressed against her stays when she lifted her arms. She winced at the soreness.

The atmosphere inside the coach was stifling. It smelled of leather and tobacco and old sweat. As the horses moved off with a jangling of harnesses, Jehanne tried to open a window and let in some air, but both of them were jammed. She closed her eyes and sagged back against the seat. The handkerchief clutched in her hand was already sodden with her own sweat.

The only other occupant of the carriage, a strong country lad, had fallen into a half doze. Jehanne opened her eyes and studied him. He was sturdily built, with great shoulders and thick muscular thighs. He had a coarse, honest face under a shock of untidy fair hair. The colour of ripe wheat, she thought, and so it should be, for a farmer.

Jehanne drew in a sudden breath against the pain in her breasts. It had been a whole day since she had given milk and they were hard and engorged. A trickle of sweat ran down her cleavage. She mopped at it ineffectually, flapping the wet handkerchief in the vain hope of creating a cool breeze.

Outside the coach, the countryside sped past.

Acre upon acre of forest, which gave way to the bright patchwork of fields. Now and then she saw an expanse of acid-green where hop fields stretched away into the distance. Farmhouses nestled in folds of land, their walls washed with pastel pinks, blues and yellows. Looking at them, Jehanne felt a surge of longing.

It would be early morning before they reached the village where she was to take up her new position. If only it was not so hot and airless in the coach. She might have slept, but for her discomfort which was growing with each passing moment. The heaviness in her breasts had become a throbbing bruising ache. Her situation was desperate. Somehow she must relieve the pressure.

She glanced again at the sleeping farmer. His head had fallen back and his mouth was open. He snored softly.

Deciding all at once, she fumbled with the fastening of her bodice. Her low-necked chemise was wet around her nipples where the milk had leaked. The tops of her stays dug into the under-swell of her swollen breasts, chafing and reddening the taut flesh. With savage eagerness, Jehanne pulled her bodice open, unable to bear the sore heaviness a moment longer.

'Ah, thank God,' she murmured as she unhooked the top of her stays and her breasts sprang free.

She dabbed at her exposed skin, rubbing her

fingertips in soothing circles over the warm, sticky flesh. Sweat beaded her top lip and she could feel the heat prickling all over her body, but the pain in her breasts had eased somewhat. She sighed deeply and lifted her head, palming the leaking nipples.

And found herself looking straight into the open eyes of the young farmer.

In confusion she looked away, plucking at her bodice as if she would draw the open garment to cover herself. But it was too late. He had seen. She chanced a look at him and saw that he was watching her steadily with something like understanding on his big-featured, plain face.

'Can I help?' he asked quietly after a moment.

Shocked, she did not know how to reply. Did he understand what was wrong with her?

'My sister has a new babe. I know how it pains a woman when her breasts are full and the babe won't feed.'

His voice was soft, his expression kindly. A sharp pain shot through one of her nipples. Jehanne barely suppressed a wince. She looked at him again. There was nothing of guile in his expression. Making a decision, she nodded, her eyes downcast, while a flush rose to stain her cheeks. Let him make the move. She was unable to give voice to the words, to ask him for what she needed.

The young man moved towards her and dropped to his knees. With trembling fingers

Jehanne cupped one of her breasts and held it up towards him. The white skin was fretted with blue veins, the nipple prominent, pushed out by the pressure of her milk, and as brown as bark.

The young man bent his head, hesitating for a moment more.

'So beautiful,' he murmured, then he opened his mouth. Jehanne placed the nipple on his tongue and he closed his lips.

He sucked gently, his mouth warm and careful of her. The pressure did not ease. After a few moments Jehanne shifted uncomfortably against his lips. He freed the breast and looked up at her.

'What is it? Am I doing it wrong?' He looked so eager to please.

Jehanne smiled, charmed by his gauche demeanour. She no longer felt self-conscious and seemed to have found her tongue.

'Well now. I expect that you're long out of practice. It's some time since you were a babe in arms. Let me help you.'

The practical side of her nature rose to the fore. Having given herself over to the situation, it felt natural for her to take charge.

'What is your name?' she asked.

'Hamish. Hamish Sawyer.'

She told him her name. 'Then let us be comfortable, Hamish. And I'll show you what to do.'

Hamish took off his rough tweed jacket. Under it he wore a striped workman's shirt. It was well laundered, but faded and frayed around the collar band. The scent of his strong young body reminded her of elderflowers. Jehanne settled down on the floor of the coach, bunching up her parcel of spare clothes to form a backrest for herself.

'Now then. Lie at my side. Settle in the crook of my arm. That's the way. And take the whole of the nipple into your mouth, not just the tip. Use your tongue to press it against the roof of your mouth. Now, suck hard. You need not be too gentle.'

Hamish did as she told him and gave a practice suck. 'Like this?'

Jehanne felt the tingling which meant that her milk was ready to flow. 'Ah, yes. Just like that. That's perfect.'

Jehanne closed her eyes as the sweet drawing down of her milk began. Having mastered the technique, Hamish sucked lustily, swallowing great warm mouthfuls with audible enjoyment. The full breast was pressed tight to his mouth. Jehanne's other breast wept with sympathetic pleasure, the pearly drops rolling down her white skin. She was embarrassed and made a move to reach for a cloth to staunch the flow.

But Hamish made a sound deep in his throat and reached out a hand. He stroked the leaking nipple gently, letting the milk roll over his fingers. He seemed completely at ease. Jehanne relaxed. As Hamish's mouth clamped more firmly against

113

her, she let out a long breath of satisfaction. It was quiet inside the coach, but for the subtle wet sounds of Hamish's mouth.

After a while he paused in his ministrations, looked up at Jehanne and smiled. A thin trickle of her bluish milk threaded from the corner of his mouth. Just like a baby, thought Jehanne, as she wiped his mouth clean with the heel of her hand.

'Is it good?' she asked him mischievously.

'So warm and sweet. I did not expect it.'

In a short time Hamish emptied one breast. They changed position so that he could begin on the other. Partly due to the heat in the coach and partly because of her feeling of well-being, Jehanne began to feel drowsy. Her head slipped backwards and she fell into a slight doze as Hamish's warm mouth worked away at her. While he sucked on her full breast, he reached up to gently knead the other one, now slack and pear-shaped.

The coach rumbled along the stony road, its interior filled with the warm milky smell of her and with the spice of their joint body heat. All at once a new sensation brought Jehanne rushing back to full wakefulness. There was a ticklish pleasant feeling in one of her breasts. Satiated and full, Hamish had drawn away a little and was licking and nibbling at her drawn-out nipple.

Jehanne smiled, completely at ease. Indeed, Hamish was like a child – though he might be a hulking great young man – a child who has fed well and is inclined to playfulness. Well then, let him nuzzle and suck at her a little. She did not mind. At first she lay back indulgently, feeling quite detached from the situation as Hamish tongued the now soft teat.

He has a nice mouth, she thought, though his face is unremarkable and verging on the coarse side. Then, as he kept up his attentions, nipping gently at her with relaxed lips and using his hands to cup her softened breasts and roll them together for his pleasure, she began to feel something. A coil of heat gathered in her belly.

Now Hamish sucked again, drawing strongly on the slack flesh. Filling his mouth, he parted his lips and allowed a mouthful of milk to trickle between her breasts. It ran down onto the upper part of her ribcage, exposed by the open front of her stays. He bent his head as if to lick up the spillage and made a little sound of dis- appointment.

'Oh, I cannot reach to clean you,' he said innocently. 'Will you unfasten your stays a little?'

Jehanne's breath came faster as she did as he asked. Why not? He had helped her and she was grateful. Besides, the feel of that naughty warm mouth on her skin was doing something wonderful to her. The bones of her stiffened basque creaked as she loosened the laces.

'There, you can reach now,' she said.

For a few moments Hamish licked at the skin exposed by her open stays. There were red marks where the whalebone had pinched. Hamish ran the tip of his tongue over the imprinted flesh. Jehanne shuddered at the unexpected delicacy of his touch. It was both soothing and arousing. She could not remember when she had so relished the touch of a man.

'You could take off your skirts,' Hamish said shyly. 'It would be cooler that way.'

Jehanne did not hesitate. 'Help me then. My skirts are heavy.'

Hamish fumbled with the fastening of her waistband. She let him open her skirts, then untie the cord that held up her petticoats. As he pushed the thick bunched fabric down over her hips she lifted a little to help him. She wore no drawers and was naked under her skirts.

She would have liked to be more beautiful for this eager young man. There was a slackness at her belly and pale, silver scars across her hips, but Hamish seemed not to notice.

'God. Oh, God,' he murmured, running trembling fingers over her soft white thighs, then trailing them lightly across the frosting of hair at her groin. 'You are so lovely, Jehanne.'

The wonder in his voice touched her. He was such a mixture of gentleness and brute young strength. Could it be that he was sexually innocent?

'Have you never had a woman, Hamish?' she said gently.

He hung his head and would not look at her for

a moment. When he spoke his voice was low and filled with longing.

'Never. But I want you badly. Will you show me what to do?'

Jehanne felt flooded by emotion. It was a curious mixture of power and humility and affection. It seemed right that they should lie together. She wanted him too – her whole body was crying out for fulfilment. And it would be a payment of sorts – she had no money, after all. An honest transaction, she thought, smiling.

Drawing him close, she cupped his face, feeling the stubble on his coarse skin. She fingered his strong, square jaw, looking into his eyes. They were hazel, with flecks of copper-brown around the irises. Pressing her lips to his she kissed him deeply. His lips were firm and he tasted faintly of tobacco. Hamish moaned against her mouth. Her blood seemed to catch fire at the simple, raw sound of his passion.

Reaching down to the flap of his moleskin breeches, she unbuttoned him and took his strong young cock in her hand. He was breathing quickly and it would soon be over if she did not manage him carefully.

'Lie down, Hamish. Be patient now. It will be good for us both this way. I promise.'

When he was quieter and lulled by her kisses and slow caresses, she opened her thighs to him and told him to lie between them. He did so, content for her to take the lead. The smell of her

117

rich female musk and the spice of heat rose between them.

'Is this the scent of all women?' he asked in wonder.

She nodded. 'Does it frighten or repel you? Not all men savour it.'

'Nay. It is wonderful. Like the earth or new bread. I have never seen a woman's quim up close. May I . . .? Will you permit me to . . .?'

'Yes,' said Jehanne. 'Look your fill. Do what you will.'

Hamish spread her sex, his movements gentle as he gazed at her. Jehanne steeled herself to lie still, but it was difficult not to arch her back as he tentatively stroked her. He obviously did not realise that he was giving her pleasure as he explored her moist folds with the roughened tips of his thick fingers. His innocence, coupled with unselfconscious enthusiasm, was a potent lure to her senses.

As he bent and took a first delicate taste, Jehanne marvelled that such an intimate act should seem natural to him. Many of her lovers had not dreamt of such a thing and others thought it demeaned them. She found herself beginning to breathe faster and had to bite back a groan as he used his mouth and tongue as he had done when suckling her earlier.

Wrapping her fingers in his thick flaxen hair, she urged him on to keep licking as her pleasure grew. Her flesh grew slick and swollen under his touch. By accident, it seemed, he pressed gently against the firm bud of her pleasure, lolling his tongue back and forth against the tiny hood of flesh. Her climax built swiftly, taking her by surprise. As she crested, then broke, she rubbed herself urgently against his mouth, gasping and crying out as the waves consumed her. The aftershocks of her orgasm ebbed finally and her body quelled.

Hamish moved up her body and kissed her, so that she tasted herself on his mouth. She felt the blunt head of his cock at the entrance to her sex. Placing her hands on his buttocks she exerted a gentle pressure, but he needed no urging. She was wet and ready for him and raised herself to receive him. He pushed into her, giving a loud groan as he buried himself to the hilt.

Jehanne raised her legs, giving him deeper access. He bucked against her, his potent young flesh sliding deliciously against her vaginal walls, making her feel tight and new again. Incredibly she felt a second climax building. She cried out and all at once she was sobbing with the deep pleasure of it, her cleated flesh pulsing around the thick stem buried within her.

Hamish's face screwed up into an expression of surprised delight. His mouth opened wide. With a hot gush, he emptied himself inside her. Jehanne held him while he thrashed and spasmed and finally grew quiet. In a while he raised his face and smiled down at her.

'You did not have to show me everything after all.'

She smiled tenderly. 'There is nothing anyone can show you about being a man.'

'I did well?'

'Oh, yes,' she breathed. 'More than you know.'

He kissed her again, with affection and pride, his rough hands stroking her hair and cupping her chin.

As the coach sped on, swaying and rumbling across the countryside, day gave way to night. Moonlight silvered the tops of trees and hay-ricks. A vixen's harsh ghostly call echoed in the night. Inside the coach, Jehanne and Hamish slept in each other's arms. Near morning, when the dawn glow lit up the thatched roofs of a village, the coach drew under the stone archway of the inn's courtyard.

Fully dressed now and composed, Hamish helped Jehanne down from the steps and handed her the parcel of clothes. Jehanne shivered as a cool breeze played about her bare ankles. Hamish leaned out of the open coach door as she stood on the cobble-stones of the forecourt. Jehanne looked up at him, lost for words. Now that they were to part, she was suddenly shy. What was there to say, except goodbye? But it did not seem enough. She tucked a lock of hair inside her straw bonnet and tied the ribbons firmly under her chin.

In the near distance, in the road, she could see

the farmer – her new employer – sitting atop his cart, waiting for her. His figure was a shadowy bulk, topped by a shapeless hat.

'I'm to be married. Next month,' Hamish blurted suddenly, as if by disclosing this secret he had given her a treasure. 'My wife-to-be has a farm and a babe newborn. Her husband was killed a year since.'

Jehanne smiled, a trifle sadly. Then she recovered herself. 'I wish you every happiness. Your wife is a lucky woman.'

'I live in the next village. It's but a day away by cart,' he said. 'We'll be neighbours. Perhaps . . .'

The coachman cracked his whip and the team of horses began to move off, their breath steaming in the chill morning air.

Jehanne stood and waved. 'When you need a wet nurse, you'll find me here,' she called.

Hamish smiled and waved jauntily. But she did not know whether he had heard her over the clattering of the horses' hooves.

War Story

'THE BAND DOWN at the Palais is supposed to be ever so good,' Monica said, shouting over the noise of the munitions factory. 'You should come out with me tonight instead of sitting at home brooding night after night. Your Ken shouldn't expect that of you.'

Hazel Price smiled and tucked a few stray fair hairs back into her headscarf. 'He doesn't. He's not dull really, not when you get to know him. It's just that it wouldn't be right. We only got engaged on his last leave.'

'Where's the harm in a few dances, a few drinks? Most of the girls have sweethearts in the forces, but they go out. Oh, say you'll come, do.'

Hazel glanced across at Monica, whose big bosoms pushed against the buttoned front of her overalls. There was a smear of grease on her good-natured face. Monica was considered to be brassy by some of the other girls, but Hazel found her lively and amusing. Before she knew it she had agreed to go out dancing.

'I'll call for you at seven,' Monica said. 'It'll be a lark, you'll see.'

Now hurrying down the road towards the bus stop, Hazel felt a mixture of excitement and reluctance. She drew level with a florist's shop, the window criss-crossed with sticky tape to prevent glass flying out if a bomb should land nearby. Despite her lateness Hazel glanced in, admiring the floral buttonholes on display. The bunches of snowdrops and anemones were pretty, but one in particular caught her eye. A beautiful white camellia, just like the actresses in Hollywood films wore. One of those would liven up her shabby dance dress.

She loved to dress up and wear nice things, but Ken said that it was vain and foolish when so many people had to make do. Still, he was proud of her slim figure and shapely legs. He called her his Betty Grable. Everyone said that she and Ken were the perfect couple. And he was what she wanted, wasn't he? Well set-up, reliable, honest, even if he could be a bit pompous at times.

She tried to conjure the image of his face in her mind. It alarmed her that she could hardly remember a thing about him, not the feel of his hair nor the smell of his aftershave. Perhaps if there had been more . . . contact between them. But Ken said it was a sin to do that thing before marriage. That was right and proper, of course. She felt guilty for wanting more.

One Christmas after too many sherries, he had pushed his hand up under her jumper and fondled her breast over her brassière. Shocked and ashamed by the warm melting feeling between her thighs, she had pushed him away. He had apologised and she had not dared to ask him to touch her again. But oh, how she had longed for him to stroke the inside of her thigh above the top of her much-darned stocking, to slip his hand inside the loose leg of her cami-knickers.

The heat rose into her face as she recalled how, later, in the quiet and dark of her own bed, she raised her nightie and touched herself between her legs. The fleshy folds there were wet and swollen. When she stroked and rubbed the bump inside the pouting little slit she had felt all tingly. Guiltily she had jerked her hand away. Nice girls shouldn't have those urges.

Hazel gave a guilty start, suddenly remembering where she was. She felt all hot and bothered and wondered if her thoughts showed on her face. The shop girl inside the florist's looked quizzically out at her. Hazel coloured, realising that she had been staring blankly in at the window for some time. Oh, crikey – the bus! Whipping around she almost collided with an American soldier as he walked into the flower shop.

'Sorry,' she mumbled, pushing past him with hardly a glance. She noticed only that he was a G.I. and tall with dark hair. She was breathing hard when she joined the queue at the bus stop. A few seconds later the bus drew to a halt. Hazel moved forward ready to board it.

'Pardon me, ma'am,' came a voice at her shoulder.

Hazel turned. The tall American G.I. held out a floral buttonhole. 'I wonder if you'd accept this,' he said. 'I saw you admiring it. I'm not trying to be fresh with you. It's . . . well. It's just that this is a great country. You English are such darn nice folks.'

Hazel's face registered her shock. It was the white camellia. How had he known which one to buy? 'I . . . No. I couldn't possibly . . .' she began, grasping the rail, ready to jump onto the bus.

A gentle hand on her arm restrained her. 'Please take it. I'd look pretty foolish with it pinned to my jacket.'

A woman standing on the bus platform looked back at Hazel and raised her eyebrows. The bus conductress looked from Hazel to the American. 'Well, miss? You coming aboard or staying here for the duration?' she said.

'I'm . . . I'm coming,' Hazel stammered, her instincts telling her to ignore the soldier. The blind cheek of him! All the Yanks were the same, flashing their money about, expecting a girl to fall right into their arms. Well, she wasn't the sort of girl to have her head turned by flattery.

She looked at the G.I. closely for the first time. He had a nice face, with regular features. His straight mouth was parted in a grin. There was an air of sincerity about him that was very attractive. Despite her reluctance she found herself smiling back. She reached for the buttonhole. 'Thank you. It's a kind gesture.'

He lifted his hat. 'A pleasure, ma'am,' he said, before turning on his heel.

The bus conductress gave a theatrical sigh and rang the bell. 'Yanks,' she said under her breath. 'Overpaid, overfed, oversexed, and over here!'

The downstairs passengers laughed at the popular cliché. As the bus pulled away, Hazel found her way to a seat. How extraordinary. She had no idea who the American was and was not likely ever to see him again. But his elegant gesture had brightened her day. She brought the camellia to her face and took a breath of the fresh sweet scent. These sort of things didn't happen in real life. They belonged in films. Just wait until she told Monica.

Later that night, when she and Monica stepped into the dance hall of the Palais, the band was playing a fair approximation of Glenn Miller's 'In the Mood'.

'Ooh, I love this tune. Don't you?' Monica said, wiggling her shoulders so that her full breasts jiggled provocatively.

Hazel agreed that she did – the sound of brass

126

instruments always caused a shiver to run down her spine. Her feet began tapping in time to the music. The floor bustled with dancing couples and the air was filled with the scent of warm bodies, perfume, and cigarette smoke. She smoothed her hands down the front of her dress, feeling self-conscious.

'What if no one asks us to dance?' she whispered to Monica.

Monica rolled her eyes. 'Don't be daft. With regiments stationed all around the county there's three blokes to every girl here! Give it a mo. We'll be fighting them off!'

Almost immediately two Polish soldiers appeared at their side. 'You like to dance?' they asked.

'Don't mind if we do,' Monica said, grinning archly. 'Come on, Hazel.'

Before she could answer Hazel found herself swept onto the dance-floor. After each dance finished there was someone else waiting to partner them. The dance hall, draped festively with flags and swathes of coloured fabric, buzzed with the sound of accented voices. They danced with British and Norwegian soldiers who bought them drinks and produced photographs of their families back home. When pressed to dance again, Hazel refused, smiling. 'I'll just sit and catch my breath first. You go on, Monica.'

'I'll stay a minute or two,' Monica said, winking at Hazel to indicate that she did not intend to spend the whole night with the first men who paid her attention. As the soldiers moved off to find other partners, she said, 'Glad you came now, aren't you? You're much too pretty to shut yourself away.'

Hazel nodded, sipping her drink. Monica was tipsy. Her laugh was a bit loud and raucous, but Hazel didn't mind. She felt happy and light-hearted. This was just what she needed. She was tired of the drudgery of war-time. Five years it had lasted, so far. Like many others, she couldn't remember the last time she had slept the night through without being woken by sirens.

Suddenly she spotted a tall figure making his way through the crowd towards her. At the sight of him, her fingers relaxed on her glass. She almost dropped her drink. 'Oh good heavens,' she hissed. 'Monica. It's him!'

'What? Who?' Monica said.

'The G.I. I told you about. The one who . . .'

At that moment the American reached her table. He grinned. 'Well, this is a surprise. Hello again. I see you're wearing the corsage. It's very becoming.'

'I er . . . Yes,' Hazel stammered. 'It's lovely.'

Monica nudged Hazel in the ribs and hissed out of the side of her mouth, 'You didn't tell me he was gorgeous! He could be Robert Taylor's brother! Ask him if he's got a friend.'

'Monica, shush!' Hazel felt her cheeks burning.

The American grinned. 'That's okay. Sure I've

got a friend. Hey Barney, come on over here and meet this pretty lady.'

Monica fluttered her eyelids at Barney as he took a seat next to her. He was fair, fresh-faced and cheerfully brash. 'Hi, sugar. What's cookin'?' he said, putting an arm around the back of her chair. Monica pursed her lipsticked mouth, edged close to the brawny G.I. and nudged him in the ribs. 'Well hello, Barney. What's your friend's name then or hasn't he got one?'

The tall American chuckled and leaned on the back of Monica's chair. Although he addressed her friend, his eyes sought Hazel's face. 'Say, we haven't been introduced. I'm Angelo. Angelo Gallone. And you are?'

'Monica. The shy pretty one's Hazel. She doesn't say much. She has hidden depths.'

Mortified by her friend's forwardness, Hazel stood up. She wished her skin was less fair. Her face must be like a beetroot. 'Would . . . would you like to dance?'

'Sure thing.' Angelo took Hazel's arm and led her onto the dance-floor.

Hazel found herself held firmly and led expertly around the floor. Close to, Angelo seemed even taller than on their first meeting. He was broad and strongly built. Next to him she felt light and fragile, a new sensation for her. Ken and she were almost the same height.

'So. Is it true? Do you have hidden depths?' Angelo said, lowering his voice. Hazel could not help laughing. She felt a little strange. Her fingers were tingling where Angelo held them. There was an unfamiliar tension in her body. He really was very good-looking. How had she not noticed that properly at the bus stop?

'Hidden depths? Like a mill-pond. Ever so deep,' she joked.

Angelo smiled down at her, suddenly perfectly serious. 'I'll just bet you do too.' His grey-green eyes were intense. A girl could drown in those eyes, she thought.

Hazel looked away, her throat suddenly dry. What was happening to her? She was aware of every inch of her body. The bits of her that were pressed against Angelo seemed to throb and burn. His breath smelt of peppermint and was hot against her cheek. She realised that she was damp where her knickers pressed against her privates. Even when Ken had kissed and fondled her, she had never felt so ... trembly, so warm and syrupy between her legs.

To cover her confusion, she ventured a comment. 'That buttonhole ... Are you always so impulsive?'

He grinned. 'Sure. Where's the sense in holding back? You never know how long you've got left. Got to live for today. Save something for too long – you lose it.'

That was true enough. Everyone said things like that these days, but somehow, when Angelo said it, it had a different reality. An image of Ken came to mind, his features blurred and indistinct like a faded photograph. You could live your whole life waiting for something to happen, she thought. Suddenly she knew that she didn't want that. She wanted to feel alive. To experience everything, however wicked or forbidden. She was fed up with trying so hard to do the right thing.

The night whirled around her in a glitter of bright lights. With only brief rests for refreshments they jitterbugged, waltzed, jived, and did the rumba and the tango. Hazel couldn't remember when she'd had more fun. She felt as if she was walking on air. Monica was still dancing with Angelo's friend, Barney. She waved as they passed by, but Monica, gazing raptly up at the enormous blond-haired soldier, didn't notice.

'Looks like your chum's fixed herself up, huh?' Angelo said.

Hazel nodded, not really listening. The smell of Angelo, his hair oil, the newly laundered uniform, the subtle underlying scent of his maleness, was making her feel quite dizzy with desire. Her blood seemed to fizz with bubbles. As the last dance drew to a close, she felt a mixture of disappointment and anticipation.

'Landed quite a catch there,' Monica said when they went to collect their coats. 'Looks like he knows how to treat a girl. Best make the most of him tonight.'

'What do you mean?' Hazel said. 'I'm not that

131

sort of girl!'

'Don't kid yourself, we're all that sort with the right man. But I didn't mean that. Angelo's moving out tomorrow with the rest of the boys. Barney told me they're just passing through here on their way south to the airfield.'

'Angelo didn't say,' Hazel said. 'Oh, well. Easy come, easy go.'

'That's the ticket. There'll be someone else like him tomorrow.'

Despite her carefree tone, Hazel's heart plummetted. Angelo made her feel desirable, reckless. It was something in his eyes, his smile, the way he held her. Well, too bad. As she left the cloakroom her steps felt leaden. Serve her right. It was a good thing temptation was going to be removed. The sooner Ken came back and made an honest woman of her the better.

Outside, Angelo looked even more imposing in his greatcoat and peaked hat. 'What's the matter, honey? You look so glum.'

She told him what Monica had said. 'It's true,' he said. 'We're pulling out tomorrow.' He drew her away from the entrance to the Palais, then turned her towards him and tipped up her chin. She could hardly meet his gaze. His grey-green eyes glinted with contained emotion. 'Look, maybe I'm crazy, but the minute I set eyes on you I knew you were special. Oh, I suppose all the guys tell you that, huh? You're so pretty. You must have any number of admirers . . .'

'No. No I haven't. You're the first person I've been attracted to in a long time.' There was a hot pressure in her stomach. It was true. She didn't care if Angelo was leading her on. She loved the way he made her feel. If only this night could go on and on.

'I gotta a coupla hours before I have to be back at the base . . .'

'We . . . we could go for a walk,' she said on impulse, tucking her hand into the crook of his arm.

'Swell! You're in charge. So – where are you taking me?'

Hazel laughed. She felt anything but 'in charge'. 'Would you like to walk down by the river?'

The moon shed a pale silver-grey light over the open fields. They did not speak, both aware of the tension between them. It was cold, with the smoky smell of frost in the air. When Hazel shivered, Angelo put his arm around her. It seemed natural to turn into his embrace and lift her chin for his kiss.

When his mouth covered hers, she felt such a jolt in her womb that she imagined he must have been aware of it. At first his lips were cold against hers, the skin of his cheek smooth and smelling faintly of cologne. He pressed open her lips and slipped his tongue inside, probing gently at first, then exploring her more insistently as she melted against him. He tasted of peppermint gum and

Lucky Strike cigarettes. She seemed to feel the effects of the kiss right down to her toes.

Angelo pulled her into the angle of a stone wall, where they were sheltered from the cold wind. She strained against him, returning his kisses with unfamiliar passion. Lord, but it had never been like this for her. Ken's closed-mouth pecks on her lips were nothing like these hot, demanding probings. The firm tongue plunged deeply into her mouth, making her think of another, more intimate penetration.

She did not protest when Angelo unbuttoned her coat and slipped his hands inside. Nor did she pull away when she felt his touch on her bare stomach. As his hand slid upwards, the curled fingers trailing over her ribs and then moving to cup her breast, she made a small sound of protest in her throat.

'I'll stop if you want me to,' Angelo said, drawing away.

'No. Don't stop,' Hazel gulped, clutching at him. She gathered her courage. It was now or never. The next words all came out in a rush. 'I've never felt like this. I want you to do . . . I want . . . everything. Show me, please?'

His hands began their slow, tantalising stroking again. 'You're sure?'

She nodded, biting her lip as he found a nipple and began squeezing it gently. The pleasure of it made her head swim. 'What's that you said? You have . . . to live for . . . now?'

He grinned crookedly at her. She knew he was amused by the breathless sound of her voice, her untutored passion. 'Yeh. Something like that. Do me a favour, honey? Stop talking. Just relax.'

She nodded, beyond words anyway. Looking down at her, he watched the play of emotions across her face as he explored her body. Hazel found it almost unbearably exciting to have his hands on her, doing things to her which Ken had never done. She tried to hide the evidence of her pleasure, but knew that her shining eyes, flushed cheeks and parted lips gave her away. He allowed her no modesty. When she pleaded with him not to look at her he shook his head, smiling in that crooked way he had. She was actually trembling with shame and need. She did not know which emotion was the stronger.

Angelo pushed her dress up to her waist and caressed her inner thighs. His fingertips were butterfly-light on the strip of flesh above her stocking tops. She felt her belly tighten as he stroked her skin. He reached for the waistband of her knickers and pulled them down. Leaving them lodged around the top of her thighs, he sought out her moist and throbbing centre.

Hazel bit back a moan and pressed her burning face against his shoulder as his fingers parted her swollen labia. Little shocks of sensation spread outwards and upwards, fanning over her stomach and thighs. She had never imagined that such pleasure could be had from simply being stroked just there. It was nothing like when she touched herself. Angelo's hand was almost unmoving against her flesh. He used just the pad of his thumb to press and roll against the stiffly erect little bump within her slippery folds. The feeling was exquisite. She found her hips working lewdly. Hoarse sounds escaped her lips.

What must he think? She felt like a hussy. Oh Lord, it felt so good. Her wetness seeped onto his fingers and the gentle, liquid pressure went on and on. Her thighs shook as she opened them wider. Now he had a finger inside her. His mouth was on hers again and the twin sensations were too much. She could not stop the pleasure building, building – then suddenly she gave a cry and shuddered against his hand, grinding herself against his wrist as great rolling waves of pleasure spilled over her.

When she grew calm, Angelo tipped up her chin. 'You okay? That was your first time, wasn't it?'

She nodded, scarlet to the roots of her hair. Her whole body seemed to glow. So that was why people were tempted to sleep together before marriage. She felt grateful to Angelo for showing her. Reaching up she put her arms around his neck and brought his face down to hers. When they kissed again she felt the need and tension in his long frame. He had been so kind and unselfish. Now she wanted to repay him.

'Show me how to do it to you,' she murmured against his mouth.

Angelo smiled. 'Yeh? You're quite a gal. You know that?' He unbuttoned his fly and placed Hazel's hand inside his trousers.

She touched him hesitantly, fascinated by the heat and hardness of the penis which pushed against his under-shorts. She liked it when Angelo groaned. It made her feel good to know that she could do this for him. When he unfastened his waist band she closed her hand around the silken stem, moving her fingers back and forth so that the skin slid along the shaft.

'You sure you haven't done this before?' Angelo said, his breath coming in short bursts.

Hazel grinned. 'I haven't, but my friend told me what to do. It seemed shocking then. But somehow now . . .' She remembered something else that Monica told her. It had sounded vile, an unbelievable thing to do. She hadn't believed that men liked you to suck them. But now she wanted to do it.

On impulse she sank to her knees. Angelo's penis looked very red. The tip was dark and moist. His pubic hair was dark and the thick organ thrusting up from it looked potent, a little dangerous. Before Hazel lost her nerve, she leaned forward. Opening her mouth she drew the glans in and sucked it gently.

Angelo's knees almost buckled. 'Oh, God,' he said. 'Oh, yeh.'

He tasted faintly of salt. She smelled soap and the faint tang of sweat. Growing bolder she took more of the shaft into her mouth. Using her tongue she explored him, lapping at the flared ridge around the glans. Angelo moved his hips, thrusting the cock in and out of her mouth. She sensed that he held himself back from plunging deeply into her throat. His leashed passion was very arousing.

'God. Oh, God,' he said again, through gritted teeth, his hands meshing in her hair as she moved her mouth over him. 'You're good at this. You'd better stop soon. I'm going to . . .'

Not on your life, Hazel thought. She wanted to do this properly. Covering her teeth with her lips she worked her mouth down the rigid shaft, once, twice, three times. Angelo gave a strangled moan. She slid her other hand beneath his balls, cupping them, feeling the tightness as his climax approached. On impulse she pressed her hand inwards, pushing one finger into the moist crease of his buttocks. Angelo's bottom tightened and he bucked against her. 'Here it comes.'

The warm flow spurted into her mouth. Hazel swallowed the chalky-tasting fluid. She felt proud of herself. And loved the way Angelo seemed so helpless at the moment of his climax. She stood up and laid her head against his chest, her hand still encircling his subsiding penis.

They arranged their clothing and cuddled for a while, exchanging kisses in which there was passion, but also a sense of friendship and peace. Both knew that their futures were divided. The interlude, while poignant, was just an episode in the story of so many in the war. After a while Angelo walked Hazel home. They embraced at the end of her road, oddly formal at the moment of parting.

'Goodbye, Hazel. Thanks for a great night,' he said. 'The memory will keep me warm on the way south.'

'Goodbye, Angelo. You take care,' she said. She watched him walk away, feeling sad that she would probably never see him again. As she walked the few yards to her garden gate, she saw an image of Ken in her mind.

Extraordinary how clearly she saw him now. She felt a rush of affection for him. It was only weeks until his next leave. When he came home she would make sure he had some rather special memories to take back with him. After all, you had to live for the moment. Some things were just too good to deny yourself.

Domia

THE CARD FABIENNE found in Howard's pocket bore one word.

Domia.

The print was gold and the embossed card of good quality. She turned it over. On the reverse side was the address – 14 rue St Honoré.

So Howard did have someone. She had expected as much. His excuses for being late for their dates had been growing more feeble. Fabienne's chin came up. The eyes which stared back at her from the mirror were cold with fury.

She knew that she looked good. Damned good. Her face was pale under the stylishly cut black hair. The subtle make-up suited her – understated eyes, full lips outlined with pinkish-brown pencil. No lines yet on her face, breasts still high and firm, legs long and slim. Men stared after her in the street all the time. Howard saw how they looked at her, their eyes avid but regretful. He liked men to look at her. She was not for them.

It was all for Howard. So why this?

He had phoned earlier that evening to cancel their dinner date. His voice on the answerphone, explaining that he had to work late, had been falsely bright.

'Sorry, darling. I'll call by the flat early tomorrow. Take you out to breakfast at our favourite restaurant. Okay?'

Fabienne scrunched the card into a ball and threw it across the bedroom. No it bloody well was not okay!

Howard would be with her now. Domia. It sounded Italian. Maybe she was a high-class whore. Someone young who would flatter him and do all the things he liked. Moan in the right places. Italian girls could be beautiful when young, but they soon grew fat, she thought bitchily. All that pasta and rich sauce.

Furiously she pulled a black silk sheath over the expensive lacy underwear that Howard liked. Steady now. She did not want to tear the dress. Howard wasn't worth it. She slipped her feet into zipped ankle boots. Sweeping her long black hair back from her face she clasped it at the nape and reapplied make-up.

A different look. Pale face, strong eyes with black liner, red lipstick – the shade of ripe cherries. Moments later she slammed the front door and ran down the steps, her black velvet cloak fanning out behind her.

As the taxi crawled through the warren of streets, Fabienne watched the traffic pass in shining streaks, headlights reflecting off wet roads. Shop windows gave onto a park and there were the spires and turrets of the cathedral. She loved the tall building with its Gothic arches and huge brooding buttresses.

The address on the card was in the old Latin quarter. As they approached the area, which although run-down had a tawdry charm, Fabienne's lip curled. Howard had always fancied himself as something of a bohemian.

'Stop here, please,' she ordered the driver.

'You wish me to wait? It is not safe for a lovely woman to be alone.'

'No. Thank you,' she said, tipping him well because he was young and handsome, yet thoughtful of her safety.

Trees lined the street. The gutters were awash with litter. Crumbled cigarette packets floated like boats down to the drains. The air smelled of rain and car exhausts. City smells. The houses had narrow fronts, closed shutters.

She turned into an alley, lit by a single cast-iron street lamp. Her heels clattered on stone cobbles, noisy in the silence all around. She glanced uneasily behind her, half regretting her decision to dismiss the cab driver. No need to be fearful. She was simply spooking herself. Slowly she walked forward. Halfway down the alley, in shadow, she saw a black-painted door with number 14 in red enamel letters. Above the door was a neon sign.

Domia.

Fabienne laughed aloud. Domia was a club – not a woman. Then why the secrecy? She hesitated for a moment only. What the hell, she had come here to find out. Pushing open the door she stepped inside.

It was very dark. Candles in sconces flickered on red velvet walls. Scented smoke filled the room. Suspended from the ceiling, a sequinned ball cast motes of light over the people who sat around. Mostly men sat at the tables which were clustered around a circular stage.

Two women sat on high stools near the bar. One in fishnet and leather, the other wearing a rubber dress, so tight that it showed every line and curve of her body. Both women were young and beautiful. They looked at her with doe-eyes, smiling slightly.

Tight-lipped, Fabienne returned their smiles. She glanced around. She could not see Howard. Perhaps he would be along later, when he finished work or whatever it was he was doing.

She liked the place, the air of expensive rather run-down seediness. There would be a show later, she thought, a striptease. Or maybe a live sex show. Two sad people humping and sweating under harsh lights – no more a turn-on than the display on a butcher's slab. Cheap thrills.

'You're showing your age, Howard,' she murmured under her breath. She couldn't wait to see his face when he saw her there. She ought to get plenty of mileage out of this. Oh, how she would make him grovel and beg before she forgave him this time.

A couple came into the club. Fabienne smelled expensive perfume, saw the glint of jewellery. Diamonds, emeralds. Her discerning eye told her that the gems were real. The women wore designer clothes, daring and beautifully cut. Leather with studded straps and black net that revealed more than it concealed. Gaultier, probably. Next came a number of men wearing dinner suits, as immaculate as penguins. One of the men was a high-up in publishing. She recognised him from a magazine.

Not wanting Howard to see her as soon as he came in, Fabienne headed for a dark corner. Someone seized her by the arm and spun her around. Amused, she turned to see a young man dressed all in black, buckles and straps across his chest. He had a beautiful face, an elegant, toned body. Gold rings glinted at his ears and in his nose. His hair was fashionably short in what the Americans called a buzz-cut.

'You're late. I'd given up on you,' he said, giving her no chance to speak. 'Come this way, quickly.'

Intrigued, she followed him through a curtained alcove. This was even better. She could watch from backstage as Howard incriminated himself. Explanations could come later. She was enjoying herself.

The beautiful young man led her down a narrow corridor which smelled of dust and grease paint. 'In here, quickly.' He opened the door, shouted inside, 'You've got barely ten minutes. Andy says to make it really good tonight. There are faces with big money out there.'

Fabienne hesitated for just a moment. Now was the time to speak up. The moment to leave. She kept silent. Stepping into the room, she saw that a woman with full blonde hair sat at a mirror. The woman turned as Fabienne entered. Her eyebrows arched in surprise as Fabienne took off her cloak and hung it up.

'Well, well. You're not what they usually send. A bit understated, aren't you? But I like the look. It's classy. Different. Are you new with the agency?'

Fabienne smiled, not yet understanding. 'Yes.'

Her heart was hammering with excitement. Why not? Howard wanted thrills. She would give them to him.

'I'm Nancy. You wanna fluff? I'm finished with the mirror.'

'Thanks. I'm Fabienne.' Fabienne sat down and began reapplying lipstick, powdering her nose.

She tried not to stare at Nancy, but it was difficult not to. Nancy was tall and strikingly beautiful. The studded collar encircling her neck threw her heart-shaped face into prominence. She wore a body harness that left her large breasts free and fitted tightly at the waist. A high-cut narrow strip covered her pubis. Her hips swelled out lusciously below the constriction of the belt.

As Nancy raised her arms to secure a black leather mask, her exposed breasts were lifted. The red-brown nipples were erect and gleaming with some kind of sparkling powder. They jutted out pertly, asking to be touched.

Fabienne felt a lurching jolt as Nancy's eyes met hers in the mirror. Nancy smiled knowingly as she pulled on long black boots and began to lace them up. Fabienne smiled back, her lips trembling slightly with a quite unexpected anticipation.

'Keep that look,' Nancy said. 'It suits you. Kind of innocent, but knowing. The punters'll like that. We're to provide a bit of fresh colour. Some new pussy. Gets them in the mood. After us it's the usual free-for-all for the regulars.'

She smoothed the fingers of her elbow-length gloves until they fitted sleekly.

'Ready?'

Fabienne stood up and turned around, her pulses hammering, suddenly aware that she had no idea what to do.

'I'll follow your lead,' she said, with a confidence she did not feel.

'Sure you will,' Nancy said. 'It'll be a pleasure to instruct you.' Leaning close, she brushed Fabienne's lips lightly with her own.

Fabienne swallowed hard. The point of Nancy's tongue had squirmed into her mouth. It had been hot, muscular. She wasn't sure how she felt about kissing a woman.

'A real pleasure,' Nancy said again, grinning confidently as she clipped the collar and leash around Fabienne's neck.

'I . . . Wait a minute.' Fabienne protested.

'Shut up. We're on.'

As they walked out onto the darkened stage, the music began. Nancy strutted along, head held high, breasts thrust forward. Her lovely face was set in a severe expression. She jerked on the leash, almost dragging Fabienne along behind her.

Fabienne was in a state of heightened tension that bordered on shock. This was not what she had expected. She felt afraid, but somehow aroused at the same time. It was a potent mixture. Two bullet beams of light flicked on, illuminating the centre of the stage. The rest of the club was in darkness. Fabienne could not see if Howard was in the audience, but she no longer cared very much. He had assumed less importance.

Nancy led her to centre stage where there was now a black leather chair with deep rounded arms and a wrought-iron rack with a selection of objects. Above it was a pulley with cuffs and restraints that could be raised or lowered at will.

'Stand on that chair,' Nancy ordered. When Fabienne was slow to obey she gave her two stinging slaps on the buttocks.

Fabienne gasped with shock and climbed onto the chair, the tight skirt of her silk dress making it difficult. Nancy ordered her to raise her arms and slip her wrists into the leather cuffs. Then she raised the pulley until Fabienne's arms were pulled up tight and she was balancing on the tips of her toes, her high heels making indentations in the leather.

Fabienne struggled to stand upright. The cuffs were padded and she was not uncomfortable at first, but soon the tension in her arms and legs became an ache.

'Please. Loosen it a bit,' she whispered.

'Now you don't really want that,' Nancy said, laughing softly. She slid her hands up the outsides of Fabienne's thighs, raising the tight skirt of the dress as she did so. Fabienne's shapely legs, in sheer black stockings, were revealed, then her lace garter belt, and finally the triangle of lace at her groin.

Fabienne bit back a cry of distress as the dress was bunched up tightly around her waist. Nancy turned her, so that she faced the back of the stage, presenting the audience with a view of her taut rounded backside, bisected by the strap of her black G-string.

Fabienne sensed the gathering tension in the club. The silence was thick. She heard someone strike a match. There was a moment of calm before she felt the slap, then her head snapped back with surprise.

Nancy placed another open-handed smack on Fabienne's buttocks. Then three more, swiftly, one after the other. Fabienne jerked as each slap connected. She bit her lips, working her hips back and forth in an effort to escape. A memory rose in her mind of being called in to the headmistress's study at her old girls' school. She had been spanked for some minor misdemeanour and recalled feigning tears to disguise the fact that she had enjoyed the punishment.

Forgotten feelings surfaced as Nancy administered a similar punishment and became her surrogate headmistress. Fabienne felt her buttocks tremble as Nancy struck them with her palm, concentrating on one at a time until they burned and throbbed. The warm pain radiated through her, sending shock waves of pleasure into her groin. When Nancy paused, Fabienne sagged, letting the pulley take her weight, her knees bouncing against the padded leather back of the chair.

Nancy bent down and took one of Fabienne's feet in her gloved hand. She lifted it high, so that Fabienne felt the strain in her knee and thigh, then she unzipped the ankle boot. She repeated the process with the other boot, placing them carefully side by side next to the chair.

Fabienne felt the leather of the chair against the soles of her feet, through the nylon of her stockings. It was warm and giving, like skin, and provided a sharp contrast to the seething heat of her bottom. The twin sensations sent a new spasm of pleasure through her.

Nancy drew the dress up higher, pulling it over Fabienne's head. Uncuffing her wrists briefly, she discarded it. Now she turned Fabienne to face the front of the stage and pushed the lace cups of the bra aside. Pulling her breasts free, she left the shaped band to cup the under-swell, forcing the exposed breasts to jut up and out.

Fabienne swallowed her protest, knowing that it would be ignored. Even if she begged, Nancy would not stop. With shiny, gloved fingers Nancy stroked her breasts, murmuring compliments and bending briefly to suck on the nipples. Fabienne felt the heat and wetness gathering between her thighs. She closed her eyes briefly, unable to contain a groan of pleasure.

Nancy's lips were warm. The sensation of sucking, the subtle pulling on her flesh, was hypnotic. The thought of all the watching eyes added to her pleasure. Then her eyes snapped open as Nancy pinched her nipples with gloved fingers. When the pressure was withdrawn, Fabienne let out a sigh. The feeling of throbbing discomfort could not be called pain. At its bitter heart there was the same poignant longing she experienced from being spanked.

Now Nancy began stroking Fabienne's breasts lightly with a flexible crop. The strokes went back and forth, teasing her sore nipples into hard peaks. Jagged flares of lust dipped down to

Fabienne's belly. She arched her back, thrusting her breasts towards the crop tip which Nancy continued to play gently across the flesh of her breasts. It was too much. She had not expected to feel this way – to feel so much. The bastion of her self-imposed repression threatened to crumble around her. She felt her eyes filling, her mouth twisting as she bit back grateful tears.

Nancy's lovely hard mouth curved with satisfaction at the evidence of Fabienne's confusion. Her eyes gleamed through the black mask. She reached down to the garter belt, slid a gloved finger into Fabienne's groin and pushed the lace triangle covering her sex aside.

Taking hold of Fabienne's pubis she tugged at the dark fleece, claiming the tight little plum with a force that bordered on cruelty. Fabienne whimpered and almost cried out. Ah, how she loved this game, this sexual sparring, this exchange of energies. It was something she had never before found with a woman. And with many men, the dominance was too crude, too pure.

When Fabienne tossed her head, Nancy crooned to her and stroked her face gently, commenting on her pretty flushed cheeks, her trembling mouth. Fabienne did not know that she wept, until Nancy caught a single tear on one gloved finger and carried it to her mouth. Their eyes met through the mask and something passed between them. Fabienne held her breath.

151

Then Nancy broke the thin sides of Fabienne's G-string and tore the lacy scrap free.

Now she adjusted the pulley, so that Fabienne could bend her knees and squat down, though her arms remained secured overhead.

'Rest back in the chair. Right back. Spread your knees and loop your legs over the arms of the chair. Come on, darling. Spread them wide. Show the punters that pretty pussy.'

Fabienne's face grew hot as she tried to do as Nancy ordered. It was impossible. She could not abase herself in public like this. Not even to get back at Howard.

But now her thighs were gripped and opened, her sex spread apart for all to see. She knew that she was wet, the inner flesh-lips puffy and swollen. Nancy stroked the dark pubic curls away from the rosy sex, exposing the inner labia and vaginal entrance to the audience. Using two fingers she began tapping the hood that covered Fabienne's clitoris.

Fabienne was swept by a riot of emotions as the subtle spanking proceeded. Never had she imagined this caress, which was both wicked and sublime. The muscles tensed in her inner thighs as she tried to drag them together, to shield herself from the eyes which watched from the darkened area beyond the stage. It seemed dreadful that her awakening must be observed, though she knew also that, but for Nancy and this accidental lesson in the majesty of dominance, she might have stayed asleep forever.

Waves of sweet submission lapped at her consciousness, making her bear down and push her sex towards Nancy's gloved hands. She thought briefly again of Howard, but now she no longer cared whether he watched or not.

Nancy raised her gloves to Fabienne's lips and pushed a finger into her mouth, so that Fabienne could taste her own smoky juices. Then she bent and began to kiss Fabienne on the soft insides of her thighs. In a moment Fabienne felt the subtle change in rhythm as Nancy bit her – not hard enough to break the skin, but enough to send ripples of new sensation deep into Fabienne's belly.

Fabienne began tossing her head from side to side, moaning loudly. She had found a new dimension within herself. All her senses, her screaming nerve ends, seemed centred on Nancy. Nancy who was so knowing, so wise, whose every considered touch, every spiked caress, sent new thrills of submission and pleasure through her.

Her arms ached with tension. The leather armchair was hot and sticky against her skin. The insides of her knees, the crease of her stretched and tender buttocks were damp with sweat. She slipped against the leather as she strained towards Nancy.

'Don't stop. God, don't stop,' she murmured, hardly knowing what it was that she was pleading for.

She felt the pleasure pooling, building. Some-one had put a tape on. Sound crashed onto her. The throbbing music filled her ears. Trent Reznor singing 'Head like a Hole'. The light from the bullet beams blinded her. Her senses were running on overload. She smelled cigarette smoke, the tang of leather, Nancy's perfume, her own arousal – salt and musk. There was nothing, no one in the world, except herself and Nancy.

'Oh, my God. Please. Nancy . . .' she sobbed as the first wrenching wave of a climax threatened to break.

As she hung on the edge, Nancy leaned over and thrust two gloved fingers deep into her. Fabienne spasmed, her hips working as she sheathed herself on Nancy's fingers. Nancy pressed her lips to Fabienne's mouth, kissing her hard, lashing her muscular tongue around the inside of her mouth. Fabienne gave a final groan and felt the vibration of it in Nancy's throat.

Neither of them heard the applause. In a dream Fabienne stood up. Her legs were shaky. She felt completely drained.

Nancy unfastened the wrist cuffs, bending swiftly to place a kiss on the inside of each wrist. She picked up Fabienne's dress and threw the crushed silk to Fabienne, who caught it and held it close.

Nancy beckoned. 'I don't need to tether you, do I? Good. Come with me.'

Swinging the collar and leash against her high

boots, Nancy strode from the stage. Fabienne followed obediently. Her thigh muscles ached and she could feel the places where Nancy had placed lovebites. She was acutely conscious of her still glowing buttocks, her sensitised breasts. Her entire body felt sore and yet more alive than ever before.

In the dressing room she looked into Nancy's eyes and smiled. Nancy smiled back, a look of complete understanding.

'You need a bath and some more attention, darling. My place or yours?' she said, taking Fabienne in her arms and kissing her with expert thoroughness.

'Mine,' Fabienne replied, returning Nancy's kiss with a newfound eagerness. 'I'm not expecting anyone. I had a date for breakfast. But I'll break it. It's not important. Not any more.'

With Kid Gloves

ON THE TRAM going home, Lily stared out of the window. A casual observer would have assumed that she was watching the scenery, but someone more astute might have noticed that her hands kept fluttering back and forth over the wrapped parcel in her lap, as though with pride or guilty pleasure.

Lily was not quite sure what had possessed her to buy the pair of exquisite black kid evening gloves. But buy them she had. They rested in the wrapped box on her lap, folded between layers of violet tissue paper. She was not a frivolous young woman, nor one given to acting on a whim. Indeed she prided herself on her common sense and level-headedness, two qualities which made her indispensable as upstairs maid to Lady Eleanor Soames.

Even now she was tempted to get off at the next

tram stop and retrace her steps to the Royal Emporium, there to hurry through the fashionable new store with its glass display cases and glittering lights, and ask to exchange the package for something more practical. What she had *meant* to buy was a pair of sensible winter gloves, hard-wearing and durable.

Oh, it was too ridiculous. She would never have occasion to wear the evening gloves – and yet she was aware of feeling happy, light-hearted. In the pit of her stomach was a warm feeling. It did not matter if the gloves had cost her a month's wages. Simply owning them made her feel special – like a lady of quality.

The tram drew to a halt and Lily alighted, the wrapped box now placed in the shopping bag along with the other purchases for her ladyship. A few minutes later she entered the imposing, red-brick townhouse by the back door. She was engrossed in her thoughts as she walked along the tiled hall to the coat- and hat-stand. Suddenly the tall figure of the butler stepped out of the shadows and loomed close, making her catch her breath with fright.

Unabashed, Samuel winked at her. 'Make you jump, did I? How's my lovely Lily today? Been out buying unmentionables for her Ladyship?' His hand slid over her skirt as he patted her bottom.

Lily's cheeks flamed, but she did not react. Two chambermaids were coming down the back stairs

157

and she was unwilling to make a scene – as Samuel well knew. Really, butler he might be, but he had no right to take such liberties in public! The next time he tapped on the door on her attic room late at night she would be sure to tell him so in no uncertain terms. Just because she had allowed him certain intimacies, that gave him no right to act as if she were a common street girl.

When the chambermaids had passed by on their way to the scullery, she flashed Samuel a pert look of disapproval in which there was still enough warmth to fan his interest. 'I had a most satisfactory trip, thank you for asking, Mr Mackey,' she said, careful to keep her voice neutral.

He hovered behind her as she took off her hat and coat. She could smell the macassar oil on his smooth black hair and the peppermint on his breath. 'How about a kiss? No one's about. Aw, come over here, Lily. Don't take on so high and mighty. Who knows better than me that you're not as cold as you make out?'

Ignoring him, she marched smartly upstairs. She did not need to look over her shoulder to know that he stood at the bottom of the stairs looking up admiringly at her swaying derrière. Although she was mildy annoyed with him, she could not deny that she was flattered by Samuel's advances. Giving in to an impulse to tease him she lifted the hem of her skirt, giving him a brief flash of her lace-trimmed petticoat and neat ankles clad in buttoned leather.

Samuel gave an audible sigh. 'You're a cruel young woman, Lily Harrison,' he said in a penetrating whisper. 'What must I do to melt your heart?'

'Oh, I'll think of something,' Lily said airily, her lips curving in a secret smile.

He was a handsome rogue to be sure, with his fair Irish skin, wavy dark hair, and startling blue eyes. At one time or another each one of the prettier maids had fallen under his spell only to be discarded when he had tired of them. Lily had other plans. She wanted Samuel Mackey, but it would be on her own terms.

Before she took Lady Eleanor's purchases through to her, she slipped quickly up to her own small room and put the box with the gloves inside on top of her pine dresser. She patted the slim box, hearing the soft rustle of tissue paper inside. Somehow she resisted the urge to take out the gloves and try them on again. That would have to wait until much later, when she had completed her duties.

She was tucking stray tendrils of her red hair into her lace cap when, from the floor below, she heard Lady Eleanor's well-bred voice raised in annoyance.

'Where *has* that girl got to? I want her to dress my hair for dinner.'

'Coming. I'm coming,' Lily muttered under her breath as she hurried down the stairs and went in to Lady Eleanor's boudoir.

By the end of the day Lily was tired and looking forward to retiring for the night. She was subdued as she took her supper in the kitchen with the other servants. Although she was aware of Samuel's eyes on her throughout the meal she took pains to give no sign that she had noticed his gaze flickering over her pale skin and abundant red hair.

As she drank her tea, she began to relax. The conversation of the other servants went on around her. She made no attempt to join in. They in turn let her be. She knew that they thought her haughty, with ideas above her station, but she did not care. She had always wanted nice things and was determined to have them. The evening gloves were an emblem of her aspirations. Samuel caught her eye and gave her one of his blinding smiles. Lily lowered her eyes. No one at the table would guess that her heart had turned over and a heat crept into her lower belly.

When Samuel looked at her like that she felt reckless, tempted to give in to her desire for him. But she knew that would be foolish. It was her coolness, her reluctance to give away more than a kiss, a hurried and stolen caress, that kept him burning for her.

Lily poured more tea, pleased that her hand was steady although her breathing was rapid, her pulses quickening. Her breasts felt swollen and heavy inside her chemise, the nipples pushing against the fine embroidered cotton. Samuel had that look which meant that he would tap softly on her door when the rest of the household was asleep. The memory of what they had shared already made her feel hot. There was a melting sensation between her legs.

Perhaps if Samuel was extra charming to her she might permit him to lift her nightgown and look at her plump thighs. Just look, mind. Once, greatly daring, she had allowed him to loosen the drawstring at the neckline of her chemise and lift her breasts free. She was rather proud of how high and round they were, the nipples as well defined as two copper coins.

How Samuel had groaned as he stroked the firm flesh, begging to be allowed to kiss them. He had pinched her nipples gently until they stood out like hard little buds – as hard as they were at this moment. She permitted herself a secret smile as she remembered the avid look on his handsome face. But Samuel was not a man to be satisfied for long with being held off. He had to be encouraged, played like a fish on a line, otherwise he would look elsewhere for more rewarding prey.

As much as she desired Samuel, Lily was determined not to go the way of the last woman he took a fancy to. Poor Maudie had been packed off back to her parents with a week's wages and no reference. That was why Samuel had to be taught some respect. She wanted to be more than his flighty piece. Oh yes, she wanted far more from him than that.

Finishing her meal, she stood up and took her used china and cutlery into the scullery. Then she said good night to Cook and the maids, nodded to Samuel and went up to her room. Her preparations for bed did not take long. She hung up her gown and petticoats, then, after washing, brushed her long hair until it poured over her shoulders in a mass of soft curls. With a gathering sense of excitement she reached for the box on the pine dresser.

The black kid evening gloves nestled between the folds of violet tissue paper. They had a softness and a sheen like velvet. There was an opening on the inside of each wrist which fastened with a number of tiny covered buttons. The elbow-high tops of the gloves were trimmed with sparkling black beads and feathers. They were so – refined, so ladylike. As Lily stroked them she felt an echo of her earlier emotion.

An idea came to her. She smiled a secret smile. Now she knew why she had bought the gloves.

It was not long before the soft tap came on her door. Lily was ready. She sat on the single high-backed wooden chair, her hands clasped in her lap, a flounced cotton dressing gown buttoned up to her neck. The room was dark except for the flickering light of a single candle.

'Come in,' she said.

Samuel closed the door softly behind him. In the small room he looked enormous, his bulk magnified by the shadow climbing the wall behind him. For a moment Lily faltered. Was it possible that she could impose her will on this man? Then she thought of the evening gloves and what they represented and was once again aware of her power – the power of women, deep and dark at heart and as old as time.

Samuel looked at her in surprise, perhaps affected by some subtlety of her expression. Obviously he had expected to find her in bed or sitting nervously on the counterpane. Her composure seemed to disconcert him.

'Lily? Is something wrong? Are you unwell?'

Lily smiled, her hazel eyes dancing. 'Oh, no Samuel. I'm very well. In fact I think everything will be perfectly all right. I think . . . I mean . . . I want us to become lovers.'

A flush appeared on Samuel's pale face. He seemed speechless at her daring. Then his blue eyes darkened with excitement. 'You want me too? Lily, darling! You won't regret this. If you knew how much I've longed for you. Watching you every day has been a torture to me. There's been no one like you. You're so cool and poised, but I knew that you burned underneath your starched skirts. Oh, Lily. All the others meant nothing to me.'

She smiled again. He probably believed that he spoke the truth. How many others had he said that to?

Crossing the room in two strides, Samuel knelt before her. Reaching out he encircled her waist and pressed his cheek to her bosom. 'My dearest girl,' he whispered. Then he became aware that beneath the cotton robe she was wearing a black satin corset. With a hoarse little groan he reached for the buttons at her throat. In a moment he had unbuttoned the robe to her waist. Unable to contain himself he reached inside and grasped her breasts, holding them together to form a deep cleavage. Then he pressed kisses all over the swollen flesh, lapping at the shadowed rift with his eager tongue.

Lily shuddered with pleasure at his touch. It was difficult to remember that she must control herself. Samuel's hot mouth closed over one of her nipples. She felt the urge to arch her back at the delicious pulling sensation as he sucked and nibbled the taut little nub. She wanted to touch herself, to cup her breasts and offer them up to him. Somehow she managed to place her hands on Samuel's broad shoulders and push him away.

Samuel looked up at her, his eyes glazed by lust, his sculpted mouth shaped into a soft 'O' of surprise. A lock of his black hair had tumbled forward onto his forehead. He looked so much like a naughty schoolboy that she wanted to laugh. He was not the imposing butler now. That was when she knew that everything would go to plan.

'Samuel – Sammy,' she said. 'You do want to please me, don't you? You want me to let you come to my room again after tonight? And for us to do all sorts of forbidden things together?'

'Yes. Oh good Lord, yes,' Samuel said in a strangled voice.

'Then you must do as I say. Downstairs you have a certain position of power. And I respect that. But here, in *my* bedroom, I'm *your* mistress.'

Samuel gulped. 'I don't understand.'

Lily chuckled softly. 'Of course not. How could you? You've had things your own way for far too long. But that's the way it's to be, Samuel. If you don't like that fact, you can leave right now. But if you stay . . .' She let the sentence trail off, pinning Samuel with a look that held desire, promise, and forcefulness.

There were beads of sweat on Samuel's top lip. His pale face was flushed high on his cheekbones. She thought that he had never looked more handsome, more desirable. For a moment her heart fluttered. Had she gone too far? If Samuel was to get up now and leave, she would lose him.

'What . . . what must I do?' Samuel said haltingly.

'What must I do, mistress?' she corrected him, hardly able to contain her exultation. He repeated the phrase by rote, putting extra emphasis on the word 'mistress'.

'Good, Sammy – I shall call you that when we're alone together from now on. Now. Stand up.'

Samuel did so. Lily rose from the chair and unbuttoned the robe from the waist down. Shrugging it from her shoulders, she dropped it to the floor then stepped out of the crumpled

165

folds. Samuel caught his breath as she stood before him clad only in the black corset, which left her breasts bare, and black woollen stockings held above her knees by frilled garters. When he would have reached for her again, she shook her head. 'Wait there.'

Turning her back, so that he was treated to a view of her generous naked buttocks, she took the black kid gloves from the pine dresser and began pulling them on. She faced Samuel now, as she fitted the supple black kid to her lower arms, sliding the fabric down each of her fingers in turn, then smoothing the rippled folds up to her elbows until each glove fitted snugly. Samuel watched avidly, unable to take his eyes from her. She held out her hands, palms up, for him to fasten the covered buttons.

With a hoarse moan Samuel grasped her slim wrists and brought them to his mouth. Pressing his lips to the slitted openings he kissed her white skin, touching his tongue-tip to each bluish vein, each bounding pulse. Lily shivered, feeling the wetness gathering at the folds between her legs. She had never been so aroused, never felt so strong and womanly.

'Fasten the buttons, Sammy,' she said after a few moments.

Samuel did as she told him. He seemed mesmerised by the black silkiness of the gloves which looked startling against her fine-grained skin. She sensed his reluctance to let go of them. Gently she pulled away. 'Now, Sammy. Strip to your drawers.'

Samuel blinked in astonishment. 'But I can't. Not like this. You . . . you're not going to watch me?' he said.

'Oh, yes I am,' she said softly, but with the slightest hint of menace. 'Surely you have no objection? Don't you know what happens to disobedient servants?'

Samuel swallowed audibly. 'They . . . they get beaten?'

'They do indeed,' Lily said, delighted to hear the note of hopefulness in his voice. 'It seems that I must give you your first lesson. For I expect to be obeyed at once, without question. Now – disrobe!'

Samuel flinched as her voice cracked like a whiplash. Hurriedly he slipped off his boots, unbuttoned his braces, shirt and trousers and laid them aside. His vest and socks followed. Soon he was clad only in his linen under-drawers. He stood slightly hunched over, his hands hovering at his groin trying to shield his huge erection.

Lily chuckled inwardly as she stepped forward, grasped his wrists and placed them firmly at his sides. Samuel's stiff cock tented the fabric of his drawers, nudging at the buttoned opening as if eager for escape. She had never seen him wearing anything less formal than his butler's uniform and had been unprepared to find his body so well-made. His shoulders were broad, his chest deep with a sprinkling of dark hair, and his stomach was ridged with muscle. Lord, but he was as fine a figure as the huge navvies who worked on the canals.

She touched his chest, moving her gloved hands over his biceps, then stroking down to where the dark hair grew in a point up to his navel. It was odd, exciting, to be touching him so intimately, but to feel nothing through the black gloves. Samuel breathed fast, his belly tautening as she trailed her gloved hand down to his waistband and slipped inside.

'Oh, Lord,' Samuel gasped, looking down at her shiny black fingers.

She ran a finger up his engorged cock, then circled the firm sac of his scrotum while he arched towards her, helplessly aroused, his cheeks flaming with shame and need. Slowly she unbuttoned the opening of his drawers and drew out his rampant cock. It was rigid, deeply flushed, the cock-skin drawn half back over the moist glans. The column of flesh, rearing up from the gap in his drawers, looked almost obscene and heavily potent. Cupping his scrotum she drew his balls through the gap too.

She had an almost overwhelming desire to bend her head and taste him, flick her tongue over the swollen glans, but in a moment she had mastered the urge. Punishment he had been promised and that was what he must have. For Samuel was a man who would feed on any woman's weakness, press home any advantage.

That did not daunt her. After tonight things would be different. Tonight she felt strong, beautiful, in control – the evening gloves adding more than a touch of glamour and wickedness to her new persona.

'Turn around,' she said sternly.

He looked blankly at her for a moment, then turned around so that his muscled thighs pressed against the mattress. Deftly she encircled his waist and unbuttoned his waistband. Samuel made a strangled sound in his throat as his drawers slipped to lodge halfway down his buttocks, revealing the firm flesh of his bottom. Giving in to a devilish impulse Lily grasped his drawers and dragged them down his thighs. They slipped further, falling in folds around his ankles. Pushing gently at the small of his back, she said, 'Lie forward on the bed, Sammy. On your belly for me.'

For a moment she thought he might balk. His back straightened and there was a stubborn set to his shoulders. Then he bent at the waist and stretched himself out as she ordered. She left him lying face down for a moment, while she picked up a hairbrush from her dresser. He did not turn his head to look at her as she moved around the room, nor did he look up when she tapped the back of the wooden brush against her gloved palm. The subtle sound of wood against leather was penetrating in the silent room.

A tremor passed over Samuel's back and his

buttocks twitched as if in anticipation or fear. 'Now, Sammy,' she purred. 'This is going to be your first lesson. I do not doubt that it will be the first of many. But you will remember this one because it is special. Think of it as . . . as,' – she searched for an appropriate word – 'as a baptism.'

Raising her hand she brought the back of the brush smartly down on Samuel's left buttock. Although he flinched with surprise he did not cry out or protest. Emboldened by his response she spanked him again. Then again. Soon the punished flesh glowed pink. She admired the contrast between the as yet untouched right buttock. Samuel's fingers were clenched on a fold of her counterpane, his head buried in the folds of white cotton.

When she began spanking him again, this time on his virgin cheek, he gave a whimpering cry of eagerness. She laid to with a will, plying him with the back of the brush until both buttocks glowed a deep peony red. Her knees felt quite weak with the flooding feeling of power and excitement. As she moved, the swollen folds of her quim rubbed slickly together. A pulsing beat seemed to penetrate deep inside her.

'How does that feel, Sammy?' she said huskily. 'Have you been punished enough?'

'Oh Lord, mistress,' he said. 'Oh, please. No more . . . Don't stop . . . I mean . . .'

Lily smiled confidently. He was almost hers. 'Just a little more, I think. And I order you not to lose control. Do you hear? If you spill your jism onto my counterpane I shall have to order you back for another session just like this one.'

Samuel moaned softly, pressing his belly more closely against the cool cotton. Deliberately Lily turned the hairbrush over and brought the bristled surface down onto Samuel's sensitised flesh. He gave a muffled howl and his hips began pumping as he mashed his member between his belly and the surface of the bed. Quite out of control now he humped and gasped as Lily spanked him on both cheeks at once. Sensing that he was near to breaking she brought the brush down in a rough stroke so that the bristles scraped across the burning flesh and penetrated his cleft, spiking deliciously at his clenched anus.

'Lily, darling! Mistress! Oh good Lord!' Samuel choked, convulsing with the pleasure-pain and the indignity.

Straining backwards, he arched his back so that his reddened bottom was tipped up towards the punishment. His hips wove and he thrust shamelessly into the counterpane as if he was pushing his cock into Lily's willing body. Lily brought the brush down between Samuel's legs and stroked the bristles gently across his taut and straining sac.

Suddenly Samuel tensed and lifted his head. The cords stood out in his neck and shoulders as he spent himself, threshing and grunting in ecstasy, his hands plucking bonelessly at the quilted counterpane.

Lily laid aside the hairbrush and stood by,

171

waiting for Samuel to recover. It took a long time for him to stop twitching with after-shocks of pleasure. Still breathing hard, he pushed himself backwards onto his knees.

'Oh dear, oh dear,' Lily said sternly, looking at the creamy wet patch on the counterpane. 'It seems as if you'll have to come back for some more training. But not until I give you the signal. From now on you'll wait until I tell you that you're welcome in my bedroom. Understand?'

Samuel nodded mutely.

'One more thing. You'll treat me with the respect due to a lady – your mistress – from now on. No more bottom-pinching and stolen kisses. And no cheeky talk when others are within earshot. Any lapses and I'll deny you all favours. Is *that* understood?'

Samuel nodded. 'As you wish, Lily darling . . . I mean mistress. Might I be allowed to ask one favour?'

Lily stroked her chin as if considering his request while inwardly she was exultant. Oh, what times they would have! 'You may,' she said at length. 'Just one, mind.'

'Please will you . . . will you wear those gloves next time? You're like a different person with them on. I hardly know you. Dear God, Lily. I'm your slave!'

And Lily threw back her head and laughed. A month's wages they had cost, but they were worth more – a whole lot more.

Peep-Show

I HAD HEARD of them, of course. Grace Jones had herself been portrayed as a peep-show entertainer for a publicity campaign to promote an album, some years back now. My lover and I had made love often to one track – 'Warm Leatherette'.

But I had never seen a real peep-show. In fact, I didn't know if they still existed or were some sort of throw-back to the Sixties, like Betty Page and *Tit Bits* magazine. I had to admit that I was shocked by my lover's suggestion.

'You mean actually go to one of those places?' I couldn't believe he was serious.

A friend had told me that he'd been to one of those peep-hole affairs while on holiday in Europe. He said laughingly that someone had actually been vacuuming the little cubicle while the girl on the turntable postured and pouted for

173

the customers! But that was Europe. I didn't think we in Britain could ever be so dismissive about sex.

'Paying to watch women expose themselves. It's so . . . seedy,' I said, imagining the unsavoury darkened booths, the men in raincoats huddling in their seats, hands jiggling at themselves while their eyes were pinned to the anonymous woman on show.

Even as I protested, I felt a flicker of excitement. Seedy, yes, but also titillating.

'Isn't that the attraction?' he smiled, seeing that I was interested. 'I've heard of a place, newly opened. It's classy, the "in" place to go. There's more to this establishment than tired whores gyrating in shabby underwear for a pound a minute.'

I put my arms around him and lifted my mouth for his kiss.

'And how do *you* know what happens in these places?' I asked teasingly, feeling even more turned-on by the thought of my lover sitting in one of those dingy little booths. 'Have you been to one?'

'Of course,' he said lightly. 'I went with a group of friends from the office once, for a laugh. It was a long time ago. Before I met you.'

I didn't believe him, but it didn't matter. Whatever he did when he was not with me was none of my concern. The snatched hours, the occasional overnight stays in his stylish, riverside flat in Docklands, were crystalline moments in the ordinary landscape of my life.

His tongue slipped between my lips and I sank against him, loving the way he tasted, the way he explored my soft inner flesh with such expert thoroughness. I knew that I was going to agree to go with him. I always did what he wanted, because I wanted it too. And because he was young and beautiful. It was my pleasure to indulge him.

Soho by night has a sort of seaside town brilliance. It's as tawdry as an over made-up drag queen. I loved the spice of excitement, the smells wafting out as the doors of restaurants opened and closed, the razor cut of danger in the air. Neon signs in yellow, orange, electric blue lit up the streets and made them one long amusement arcade. Sex shops, selling plastic penises, rubber items, day-glo French ticklers and a riotous assortment of garish underwear, plied their trade like static whores.

I clung to my lover's arm as we walked, both of us enjoying the stares, the glances of startled appreciation. Maybe some of them recognised me. I could almost hear their thoughts. 'Isn't that . . . No, it can't be.' My lover was so obviously a lot younger than me, but I was still quite a catch. I have an ex-model's slender figure and good legs. The slim designer dress and high heels showed them off to advantage.

My lover pointed across Great Windmill Street. 'There,' he said. 'That's the place. Interesting, eh?'

I couldn't agree. The doorway was next to a shop which seemed to vibrate with garish neon signs. 'Striptease', 'Exotic Shows', 'Adult Videos', the signs proclaimed. And over the doorway next to the shop a similar sign glowed redly. 'Peep-show downstairs.' Was this a joke?

Despite my reluctance, my pulses quickened as I followed my lover into the darkness. Downstairs we entered a womb-like basement; red carpet, swirly red-flock wallpaper, red light. The colour bleached out the features of the haggard man sitting at the counter. My lover handed him a sheaf of notes. We passed by with a nod.

I felt the man's eyes on me and smiled at him and swung my hips. They couldn't get many women in a place like this, at least, not anyone other than 'working women'. Certainly not like me: mature, well-groomed, wearing black silk by Versace and matching, hand-made shoes.

We walked along a landing until we came to the booths. Six of them. The atmosphere was close and there was the smell of cigarettes and something else, almost antiseptic. A middle-aged man slanted me a look. His eyes slid quickly away when I smiled back without a trace of embarrassment. Some of the booths were occupied, their doors hanging open. I saw a youngish man in one. He wore a heavy overcoat and was hunched over, making small movements inside the shelter of his coat. It was what I had expected, after all.

For some reason I found it all sad and dreary.

But it was also as seedy as I'd imagined it would be and that rather excited me.

'In here,' my lover said, taking my arm and directing me into one of the booths.

It was very dark and cramped. My eyes took a moment to adjust. There was only a narrow bench to sit on. In one wall there was a window the size of a letterbox opening, covered by a metal plate. Beneath it was a coin slot.

My lover propped the door open deliberately. Now anyone walking past could look in and see us. I was unnerved by that, having always preferred to take my guilty pleasures in secret. But I did not protest. My lover never did things by accident and I wondered – what was his purpose?

For a moment nothing happened. I waited, expecting the metal covering over the narrow oblong window to be removed.

'Don't we have to put some money in the slot?' I whispered.

My lover shook his head. 'We've paid for a special show. Be patient, darling.' His fingers traced the contour of my cheek.

I leaned against him, wanting to feel his warmth against my skin. My dress was sleeveless and I shivered when he ran the tips of his fingers up my bare arm. His lips moved to my neck. They were firm, demanding. I knew what he wanted and parted my thighs.

Under the dress I wore only a black satin suspender belt and lace-topped, sheeny stockings.

I shuddered when he pushed up my dress and rested a hand on my thigh. Just then, a light went on in the room beyond and the metal covering the narrow window was removed.

Viewed through the oblong opening, there was a woman on a bed. She wore only an open-cup, lacy bra and a lace G-string. Covering her face was a frilly black mask. She was positioned on all fours. As she moved to and fro, arching her back and weaving her hips, her breasts swung lazily. The nipples poked rudely out of her scanty bra. She had a good body; firm generous breasts, slim waist, a taut curvy bottom.

A wash of pinky-red lit the room, giving a surreal quality to the woman's skin and turning the blackness in our booth to violet-toned twilight. As I watched, the woman moved to the edge of the bed. She was graceful, her movements fluid and sexy. Her curly dark hair spilled over her shoulders.

'Wouldn't you like to make love to her?' I whispered to my lover.

He didn't answer, which pleased me. In the grainy light he smiled and kissed my mouth. His fingers described tiny circles on my inner thigh and I felt the beginnings of that special ache in my sex. My nipples hardened, brushing against the cool black silk of my dress as I strained towards his hand.

When his fingers closed possessively over my pubis, I gasped, anticipating his touch on my moist vulva. I knew that I was swollen and receptive, the dew seeping out of me, but he denied me the intimacy of the caress I wanted so much. He contented himself with stroking my pubic hair, teasing the springy curls into strands. The tension coiled within me as he sat calmly watching the woman in the other room while caressing my mound with almost casual familiarity.

'Please . . .' I whispered. 'Touch me. Feel how wet I am.'

He shook his head. 'Not yet. When I'm ready.'

For a second I hated him. He was so self-assured, so certain of his attractiveness. But the feeling passed almost immediately. It was his refusal to compromise in any way which kept my interest.

Sitting on the edge of the bed, the woman raised her hands to the tips of her exposed breasts and took hold of her nipples. As she twisted them, pulling them out into little tube shapes, I felt an answering pull in the base of my belly. How deliciously painful that looked. Her nipples were large and of some dark colour, brownish-red or copper, I imagined. In this light, colours were deceptive.

With her other hand, she reached down and pushed the G-string aside. She had a lot of black pubic hair. As she began stroking herself, pushing aside the silky hair to probe her labia, I glimpsed the shadowed parting of her flesh. The red lips looked bleached by the artificial light. Her fingers were wet and she began moving her hips as she rubbed her clitoris. She seemed to be enjoying herself. If she was acting, she was good.

'Get up on the bench,' my lover whispered hoarsely. 'On your knees, bottom in the air.'

I did as he asked, feeling the narrow board under my knees, the wood hard against my stockinged shins. As the toes of my expensive shoes were bent against the hard surface, the muscles in my calves protested. Standing behind me, straddling the bench, he rolled my skirt up to my waist. The close, fusty air of the booth was soft on my bared buttocks and the tops of my thighs. Grasping the neckline of my dress, he yanked it down so that my breasts spilled out and hung down beneath me.

'Oh,' I breathed, feeling an exquisite sensation wash over me. My lover knew how I loved to take on the submissive role during our sex-play.

Now I must look like *she* had when the shutter was removed and the pink-washed room came into view. It was almost as if we had changed places.

My lover curved his body over mine and his erection sprang up between us, the length of it nudging against the parting of my buttocks. He was hot and hard. Adjusting his position he slid straight into me – so slick and smooth. His hands cupped my breasts, stroking, then pinching, and I writhed under him – loving it, loving him.

Turning my head, I watched the woman masturbating and imagined that she could look out of her narrow window to see me being fucked, my body moving in time to my lover's deeply penetrating thrusts. Would she enjoy watching us? I chewed my bottom lip as my pleasure mounted and hers seemed to follow a similar path.

Look into my eyes and see me, I groaned inwardly. My lover and I are your peep-show. But she seemed oblivious to the eyes watching her from the other booths, her entire concentration centred on bringing herself to orgasm.

'You're like hot silk inside,' my lover said, his voice distorted by passion. And I started to come.

I couldn't hold back and he knew it. He rode me hard now, the way I liked it. I spasmed and bucked against him, helpless as I dissolved and broke into splinters of pure sensation. He was so deep inside that I could feel his balls brushing my buttocks as he pounded into me. The twisting, pinching movements of his fingers on my nipples was sweet torture.

I cried out as the pleasure pulsed right through me and my inner muscles contracted around his buried shaft. 'God. Oh God . . .' I moaned.

In the other room, the woman had thrown back her head. Her face screwed into a rictus of ecstasy as she came, her fingers buried in her vagina, her thumb circling circling the glistening bud of her clitoris. I felt that she and I were kindred spirits, but I was so much more circumspect. I admired her for her total lack of inhibition.

How did it feel to know that you were the centre of attention? That every man watched you, wanted you? What a challenge it would be to find out.

My lover moaned and gave a long sigh. I felt his breath on my neck as he emptied himself into me, making the inarticulate little noises that I cherish. How special is the moment just after he has climaxed. He is so vulnerable then. I felt him growing soft inside me, but my body was reluctant to let him slip free. Turning my head I reached back over my shoulder and brushed my lips against his damp hair.

Then I froze.

For the first time I glimpsed the back of the booth, which had been partially screened from my sight by the open door. The door was closed now. I saw the second letterbox-sized slit, the darkness beyond. And in the darkness I saw the reflected points of light from the eyes – many eyes – watching me.

My lover laughed softly. 'How does it feel to have other men watching you, each one of them wanting you?' he asked. 'Each of them listening to your cries of pleasure?'

I smiled rather shakily, absorbing the fact that his words so nearly mirrored my thoughts. 'I don't know. You haven't given me time to absorb the fact that we *have* been watched. I'm too shocked to react.'

In fact I was very calm. There seemed a perfect symmetry to the situation. As he helped me sit up and straighten my dress, he said tenderly, 'It was a rotten trick to play. You're not angry with me?'

'No. Of course not. I always enjoy your games. But perhaps you should have told me about the other peep-hole. Then I would have known what to expect. It seems the fair thing to do.'

'Ah, but it was my secret pleasure to keep it from you. To enjoy you in your innocence, knowing that you belonged solely to me and they could do no more than gaze upon you. I loved knowing that only I can have you.'

Selfish boy, thinking of his own pleasure. I kissed him deeply, then bit his bottom lip to punish him just a little. The saltiness of his blood on my tongue was satisfying and his wince, the cool inrush of his breath, like a caress.

'The next time we come here I'll know that I'm being watched,' I said. 'And I'll put on an even better performance – for you as well as them.'

'You actually like it? You enjoy the thought of being watched?' he said, his voice, for the first time, unsure. Was that just a flicker of self-doubt in his fine dark eyes?

And I laughed, enjoying the shock on his beautiful arrogant face and the fact that I had robbed this wicked boy of his victory. At least – for the moment.

Charity Begins . . .

MISTRESS CHARITY PENN set down the pail of slops and wiped her forehead with the back of her hand. The sun beat down overhead and trickles of perspiration ran down her armpits and soaked into the top of her stays. Inside her woollen stockings her legs itched and prickled, but she dared not leave off the garments. Someone would be bound to notice her bare ankles.

Inside the stockade there was a rich stew of odours – wood smoke, roasting meat, horse dung, and the acrid stench from the tannery. In the stifling heat of the Virginia summer, the air was filled with the sound of toil as the settlers went about their daily work. In their black clothes, relieved only at collar and cuff by starched white lace, they looked like so many magpies.

Charity sighed, picked up the pail and continued on her way to the pig pen. Outside one of the square wooden houses, Jacob Hawkins was chopping wood, his shirt-sleeves rolled up to reveal brawny forearms. At the sight of his broad shoulders and narrow hips, his muscled thighs moving under his leather trousers, her knees went weak.

She knew that it was immodest to stare so, but she could not help it. Jacob was as near beautiful as any man got. His long fair hair was caught at the nape with a thong, but loose strands of it had escaped. Wisps of it whipped around his bronzed face as he worked and stray hairs clung to the damp skin of his shoulders. Chips of wood flew into the air as he brought the axe down squarely onto a log, splitting it so that one perfect half fell either side of the block.

The sappy smell of chopped wood seemed to her to be the most alluring scent in the world. Before she could think better of it, she found herself calling out a greeting.

'Good morrow, Jacob. Is it not a beautiful day?'

Oh Lord, she hoped no one else had heard her raise her voice. Calling out to a man like a common fishwife, that would be a black mark against her. Jacob did not seem to mind. He grinned and paused in his work. Leaning on his axe-handle, he watched her as she passed by.

'Good morrow to you too, mistress,' he said. 'Indeed it is beautiful, especially from where I'm standing.' He sounded amused by her presumption. His eyes, sweeping lazily over her, quickened with more than passing interest.

Charity slowed her steps. Perhaps she would risk a few words with Jacob. Surely the censure of the community would not fall upon her for exchanging innocent pleasantries with a young man in the good open air. She was shaping the words in her head when the sound of a harsh voice at her elbow made her start.

'Be about your business, Mistress Penn,' said Minister Barber. 'The Devil makes work for idle hands. And it would behove you to use less lace in your dress-making.'

Charity prickled with outrage, but bit back the retort that rose to her lips. The deep lace collar she wore was the work of a whole winter spent indoors when the mud was so thick inside the stockade that it was a misery even to run to the privy. She was proud of her lace-making skills and did not think God would begrudge her the chance of displaying the fruit of her labours. But the generous and loving God she spoke to in her heart seemed to be a different deity from the one Minister Barber spoke of, his harsh voice booming out from the pulpit of the church on the Lord's resting day.

'Well? Get on with you now,' the minister said. 'Go and draw your water from the well.' He made shooing motions with his hands. As if I were a mouse in the hay-rick, Charity thought, and not a young woman of marriageable age. And I'm not going to fetch water. If he had been at all interested in her, he would have seen that her pail was already full of pig food.

Although she glared her defiance, the minister did not stop to remonstrate with her but strode away, certain of being obeyed. From the tail of her eye she saw Jacob wink at her, the corners of his mouth pulling away in a wicked little smile. That made Charity feel better. She returned the smile, then without a backward glance hurried on to the pig pen.

The reddish Virginian dust rose up around her buckled shoes as she walked. As she drew nearer she heard the sound of raised male voices. In between the laughter and shouts of encouragement, there came a veritable cacophony of grunts and squeals. Puzzled, she rounded the building which screened the communal pen from view and stopped in amazement. A number of men, mostly the elders amongst the settlers, were grouped around the stout wooden fence.

Inside the pen, the sows were running back and forth in a frenzy of excitement, while the huge saddle-back boar sniffed at their haunches. One of the men leaned forward, waving his arms and shouting instructions. Through the space that opened up, Charity had a brief glimpse of the proceedings. The boar raised its head, its muddy wet snout questing the air, then it gave a throaty squeal and launched itself across the pen.

She had a brief impression of the boar's curling organ, erect and dripping, before the beast gave a lusty grunt and covered a willing sow. The reddened porcine eyes closed and the boar's teeth ground together with pleasure as it began thrusting vigorously. At the sight of the great ballocks, swollen with the fluid of generation and swaying between the boar's thrashing haunches, Charity's cheeks reddened. She knew that she ought not to look, but fascination drew her feet forward. Besides, the men were too preoccupied to notice her.

'That's it, my lusty. Give it to her!' one of the men shouted.

'Aye. Rut away! Make the sow squeal like a wench in childbed!' said another.

The ribald comments and coarse laughter made Charity prickle with embarrassment. Could these be the same men who berated any young woman for the slightest act of assumed immodesty? She felt uncomfortable being the only female in all-male company and was about to slip away when one of the men turned and saw her. For a moment he did not speak, but looked her up and down, his eyes sparking with animal lust.

Even in her innocence of men, she knew that he was aroused by the spectacle of the boar servicing the sows. His glance seemed to undress her where she stood. Inside, she cringed away from the hot, cruel eyes, but she would not lower her gaze and give the man the satisfaction of knowing that she was shamed by having been caught watching the mating. If it was considered fitting for men to watch, then why not women too? For surely in a farming community everyone knew how piglets got started.

The man nudged his neighbour. In a moment Charity found herself censured by all eyes. She felt an agony of self-consciousness and wished herself a hundred miles away, but she looked them all in the face. A silence fell. Then there were murmurs of consternation. Someone muttered, 'Disgraceful conduct!' A few of the men shuffled their feet, exchanged furtive glances. She heard someone say, 'She's but newly arrived at the settlement. Mayhap she does not know our ways.'

Before she could identify the speaker and flash him a smile of grateful thanks, another voice rang out.

'This is no place for you, mistress, nor for any modest woman.' Charity recognised the man as Josiah Wainwright, one of the pillars of the community. He was a thin man with reddish hair, hollow cheeks, and a jutting chin. 'Did you not know that all women were told to avoid the animal pens this day?'

Charity shook her head. 'I heard no such announcement.'

'Indeed? Then you should stay to listen to the minister's promulgations in church after the end of the service,' Josiah said severely. 'Instead of running off to the house of that disreputable, half-breed woman who serves the settlement as midwife!'

189

Charity coloured at the slur on her friend. Samaseta – better known by her anglicised name of Sarah – was the only person with whom she could be truly herself. Despite being looked down upon because of her Indian blood, Sarah did not judge or preach the judgement of hellfire, as did the pious wives and daughters of the settlement worthies. And she listened patiently, always answering Charity's questions with honesty.

'Berate me if you must, Master Wainwright, if you deem it necessary for the good of my soul,' Charity said coolly. 'But I would ask you not to pass comment on one who is not present to answer for herself!'

There was a shocked silence. Josiah's bony face paled. Charity lifted her chin defiantly, waiting for the explosion of righteous anger which would surely follow. Just then, the boar gave an ear-splitting grunt of pleasure. The sow he covered let out a warbling squeal and jerked forward. Sliding off the sow's back, the boar stood snorting and trembling, his still erect organ shiny and dripping. It looked shockingly red. Charity tried not to stare at it.

'He's ready for another,' one of the men said, his voice thick with admiration at the boar's prowess. 'See how his pizzle is still standing.'

'Aye, and the sows be glad of it! Look how they present themselves ready for him.'

'You'd best begone,' Josiah said in a voice that held ice. 'Lest you be corrupted by such bawdy talk. I'd advise you to pray for modesty, mistress. Aye, and you've yet to learn to afford the proper respect to your betters! I'll be speaking to the minister about you.'

'I don't doubt that you will, Master Wainwright,' Charity said pertly, dipping a shallow, almost insulting curtsy. There, let the nasty creature find fault with that! She had the satisfaction of knowing that Josiah was fuming inwardly, but he could not actually take her to task for any lack of manners. She was annoyed too that the minister had not seen fit to warn her about the mating when he spoke to her earlier.

Dumping the pail of swill at Josiah's feet, she said with laboured politeness, 'Perhaps you will see to it that my pig is fed after she has been serviced, Master Wainwright, since I am not permitted to attend her this day. No doubt she will relish her meal after her strenuous labours. I'll call back for the empty pail later when you have all gone home to your good wives.'

Smiling to herself she strode away, the sight of Josiah's furious impotent face imprinted on her mind. She walked with shoulders set and her back straight, her head held high. As the boar set up a lusty grunting, she heard the mocking laughter of the men floating after her. I hate them all, she thought. They are so secure in their superiority.

She felt in a bad temper after leaving the men and ill-inclined to go back home where a dozen or more tasks awaited her. Nothing was so pressing that it could not wait. On impulse she decided to go and visit Sarah, Josiah's words having put her in mind of her friend. Sarah's cottage was outside the stockade, beyond the fields of maize. As Charity skirted the fields of ripening corn and entered the canopy of trees, she took off her broad-brimmed hat and untied the straps of her lace cap. No one from the settlement could see her here and berate her for immodest behaviour.

The dappled sunlight on her bare head felt wonderful. She shook out her hair so that it tumbled over her shoulders in shining brown coils. The path to Sarah's cottage was well worn. At one time or another all the settlement women had need of her services. Sarah was far more than a midwife. She had knowledge of secret things – things to which men were not privy and which they would have been outraged to discover.

As Charity approached the cottage, she saw Sarah seated outside. She was shelling beans into a large basket of woven grass. Sarah always wore Indian dress. Her tunic of bleached doeskin was decorated with beads and feathers. Ebony plaits hung down to her waist. Catching sight of Charity, Sarah looked up and waved, her generous mouth curving in a smile of welcome.

'Good morrow, Charity,' she said in the perfect English she had learned at the mission school. ' 'Tis good to see you. Will you come inside and take a cup of sassafras tea?'

Charity followed Sarah into her cottage. The interior was cool and spotlessly clean. It smelled of dried herbs, jerked meat, and lamp oil. Sarah sat on a trunk which was covered by a brightly patterned Indian blanket. They spoke of inconsequential things whilst the tea was brewing. Sarah stirred honey into the tea and passed Charity an earthenware cup, then suggested that they take the steaming brew outside.

'And what's amiss with you, my friend?' Sarah said, when they were seated on the wooden bench.

Charity took a sip of her tea before she answered, looking up over the brim at Sarah's handsome face. With her shining black hair, honey-coloured skin and strong features, she was a striking woman. Charity was no longer surprised by Sarah's perception. There had been many similar incidents in the past.

'You always know when something is wrong,' she said.

'I have the sight,' Sarah said simply.

Charity found it easy to tell Sarah about what had happened at the pig pen. 'I hate those men,' she said. 'They are worse than animals. They are coarse beasts. I think that I shall never marry if I have to do that ... that ... filthy thing with a man!'

Sarah chuckled. 'You hate all men? Even young Jacob Hawkins?'

Charity smiled briefly. 'Well, perhaps not him.

He seems different. But for all I know he's no better than the rest of them in one respect. Oh, Sarah, the way they were all encouraging the boar. They were so excited by its stiff pizzle and the way it thrust itself into the sows, I saw them drooling with envy. But they tried to hide the fact when they saw me.'

'And you?' Sarah said evenly. 'Never mind the men. They're foolish and deny their own natures. Were you excited by what you saw?'

'Sarah!'

'Oh, you need not pretend to be shocked. This is me, remember?'

Charity lowered her eyes and remembered the swimming, light feeling in her stomach as she watched the boar serving the sow. 'Yes. I was excited,' she said haltingly. 'Why is that? It is wrong, is it not, for women to feel so? I know that there is no pleasure in the act of generation for us. That is why it is forbidden to speak of it. It is ugly and unpleasant. But we must suffer it because of the sin of Eve.'

Sarah sipped her tea, her hands cupped around the earthenware vessel to absorb the warmth of it despite the heat of the day. She was silent for a while as if considering her answer, then she said, 'Did the sow seem to be enjoying the boar's attentions?'

Charity nodded. 'As far as I could tell. I could not see very much.'

'Then do you not think that a woman can enjoy a man in the same way?'

'Indeed not! We are not animals to take our pleasures where we will!'

'Ah, but we are, my poor innocent. It is because there *is* pleasure to be had when man joins with woman that the act is surrounded with rules and secrecy.'

Charity was stunned. 'I cannot believe this! Sometimes, in the sewing circle, the married women make certain . . . comments. They speak of their duties with such distaste that I shudder to think of what they endure.'

Sarah threw back her head and laughed. 'Those silly geese! What a rod for themselves they make! The marriage-bed need not be such a barren country. Listen to me. I have never lied to you, have I?'

Charity shook her head. 'No. But we have never spoken with such a lack of modesty before.'

'Modesty! What's that but another of the ties that bind you? Forget all you have been taught for the present. There is the world you must live in, my friend. And there is the world inside you. In order to be true to yourself, you must discover that the two go hand in hand. We hold the secret of our own pleasure inside our bodies. Women of all times have had to open themselves to this truth in order to be happy.'

Charity was not sure she understood. Sometimes Sarah spoke in riddles. Her friend thought the settlers lived comical and unnecessarily complicated lives, but it was all very well for her to judge when she was able to go her own way. There were rumours that Sarah had a lover, an Indian brave, who visited her cottage from time to time, but who lived with his people for much of the year. Charity sighed, wishing that she understood more about men and women.

Sarah seemed to empathise with her. 'You need to see something for yourself, then you will understand what I speak of. When you leave here, do not go back across the cornfield, but make a wide circle and enter the settlement by the postern gate.'

'Why?'

Sarah smiled sagely. 'You'll find out. Only remember not to judge too harshly. Learn from what you will see. I am giving you knowledge. Use it as you will, but do not abuse that knowledge. You will understand what I mean later.'

When Charity took her leave of Sarah, a short time later, she was still puzzled. Whatever could she expect to learn by simply taking a walk through the forest? She shrugged, trusting in Sarah's integrity. As she walked she swung her bonnet and lace cap against her full skirts. The rhythm was soothing and dulled her into a mood of relaxation. Before long, she found herself enjoying the beauty of the forest.

Many of the leaves were tinged with the yellow and russet which presaged the approaching fall. Dappled light, like gold coins, coloured the forest floor and the scent of pine resin rose from cushions of slender green needles as she walked over them. The grey-brown bulk of the settlement was visible through the trees and she kept it always on her right, making certain that she did not venture too far into the wilderness where tribes of unfriendly natives dwelt.

Gradually she found herself thinking of her conversation with Sarah. Just recalling the subject made her feel hot and ill-at-ease. Whatever her friend said, she would never be convinced that there was anything of pleasure for a woman in the act of generation. Woman was born to suffer, so said the scriptures, and kick against the goad though she did, she felt at heart that this was the truth.

Her high spirits plummeted as she walked. The men would tell their wives what had taken place at the pig pen. She could imagine the sidelong looks, the expressions of righteous indignation. Well, she was certain of one thing. She would never marry, never engage in that painful disgusting act. It was only beasts and men who saw any merit in it at all.

A flash of colour and a movement between the trees arrested Charity's attention. The sound of laughter high and carefree floated to her on the breeze. She paused, surprised that there should be anyone else in the area at this time of the afternoon. Perhaps a group of children were out checking snares for conies. Then she heard the laughter again. Definitely a woman. Soon after, she heard a man's deep baritone and knew that she had stumbled on a lovers' tryst.

Slowly, taking care to move quietly and hold the folds of her gown against her legs, she advanced towards the source of the laughter.

Ahead of her, she could see that there was a glade, ringed all around with silver birches. Grassy hummocks dotted with wild flowers formed a natural couch for the two figures who reclined there. They spoke in low voices, in which there was a tension that was almost tangible. As Charity watched, the woman sat up, giving Charity a view of the man whose body she had obscured.

'My Lord! Josiah Wainwright,' Charity said under her breath.

And indeed it was he, with a look on his face she had never thought to see. His hollow-cheeked visage was flushed and animated, his flat blue eyes alight with honest lust. He smiled up at the woman, his lips curved with eagerness.

'Hurry and disrobe, Mary. I have longed for thee so and can hardly wait to tup thee,' he said thickly.

Charity's eyes opened wide with shock as she recognised Mary Barber, the minister's wife. She remembered Josiah's words to her and felt a surge of righteous anger. The hypocrite! She took a step forward, was on the point of marching into the glade and demanding to know just what was going on when something stopped her. This was no business of hers. Besides, it would be a crime to see the expression drain from Josiah's face. He looked almost handsome, and happier than she had ever seen him.

Mary too was giggling like a schoolgirl, and her a respectable married woman!

As Charity watched Josiah fumbling with the laces on Mary's woollen basque, she felt an odd fluttering sensation in her belly. It was just like the morning at the pig pen. She recognised the feeling now as anticipation. There was such an air of sexual tension and unbridled enjoyment in the glade that she wanted to see more. Just then Josiah pulled open Mary's basque and dipped both hands into the neck of her shift. With a groan deep in his throat, he drew Mary's breasts free and buried his face in her shadowed cleavage.

Mary gasped as he kissed the fat globes, pressing them together before sucking noisily at her nipples. Writhing against him, she threw back her head, her eyelids fluttering closed with enjoyment. Charity wondered how it must feel to have a man's hot mouth close over her nipple and suckle it like a babe.

When Josiah moved back for a moment Charity saw the thrusting teats which had gathered into hard, puckered buds. They were wet with Josiah's spittle and glowing like dark cherries. Josiah pinched Mary's nipples until her breath came fast and her capacious bosom heaved up and down.

'Oh, Josiah, my lusty. Help me with my skirts. I can hardly wait. I long for thee so!' Mary whimpered with eagerness as Josiah fondled her stockinged calves then slid his hand higher.

'Wait awhile, sweetheart,' Josiah said, moving his hand back and forth beneath Mary's petticoats. 'I'll make thee as slippery as an eel before I tup your sweet quim.'

'Oh, say more of that. When you talk that way, you make me so hot for you,' Mary gasped, sighing with pleasure and rubbing herself against his hand. She opened her legs wide. 'You're a wicked, sinful man with clever, lewd fingers. And I love what you do to me.'

Josiah chuckled huskily. 'Aye, and I do relish you too, my juicy dumpling. Your dimpled thighs, your white breasts, and your wonderful rosy quim are like manna from Heaven to a starving man.'

Charity could hardly believe her ears. This was not the hatchet-faced Josiah she knew. Juicy dumpling! It was laughable, but she felt anything but humour. The place between her thighs was pulsing sweetly. Her own breasts had swollen inside her dark gown and the nipples pushed firmly against her shift. When she made the slightest movement, they scraped maddeningly back and forth, sending little shivers of sensation down to her throbbing groin. She wished that a man would stroke her between the legs, like Josiah was doing to Mary. She too wanted to experience that dream-flush that made the minister's wife so pliant and languorous.

For the first time, she began to see what Sarah meant. There was one world of reality, where everyone must bow to the conventions of faith and law, then there was the inner world of personal experience. Sarah had implored her not to judge, but simply to learn. And she was doing that right enough. She had never imagined that anyone would do what Mary was doing now!

'Oh, Josiah. Enough or I shall spend. Lie back. Let me attend you now,' she said, pushing him back to lie on the ground.

Efficiently she dealt with the buttons on his leather breeches. Chuckling she ran her hand over the bulge at his groin, before sliding her hand inside the opening and pulling down his white linen drawers. With a sound like a low growl she drew out Josiah's erect member, stroking it as if it were a friendly dog. Then she bent her neck and placed a delicate kiss on the skin that covered the cock-tip.

Charity muffled a cry of surprise. Who would have thought that Josiah possessed such a fine crested cock? It had a thick shaft, all fretted with veins, and it reared up from a nest of curling reddish hair. It was all Charity could do to stay silent. She pressed her knuckles against her mouth, watching intently as Mary began licking Josiah's rampant member. After smoothing back the cock-skin with eager lips, Mary took the swollen tip in her mouth and sucked lustily.

Josiah closed his eyes, his face bound by an expression of bliss. 'Oh, Mary. You lovely wanton,' he breathed, his hips working beyond his control and his hands stroking her bulging cheeks. 'You've the lips and tongue of a Jezebel. Ah, you'd best stop soon, or I'll spend in your mouth and be of no manly use to you.'

Mary sat up. Her lace cap was askew and her dark hair stuck out all around her pretty face. Her cheeks were pink and her mouth swollen with kisses. Charity was doubly amazed. In church every Sunday, Mary Barber sat next to her minister husband, her small mouth clenched sourly and a severe expression on her face. Charity had never seen her wearing anything other than high-necked black gowns, trimmed sparsely with white, and her hair stuffed completely under a plain linen coif.

Now Mary looked like a wood nymph. If Charity had been in any more doubt about women receiving pleasure from 'the act', one look at Mary's glowing face would have convinced her otherwise. Mary lay back on a grassy hummock. With both hands she began raising her skirts. She looked gloriously wanton with her naked breasts spilling richly out of her opened basque, her stockinged legs sprawled apart. Josiah knelt between her thighs and helped roll up her skirts until they lay around Mary's waist.

Glancing down between her spread thighs, he

202

gave a groan. 'Did ever God create a more fragrantly wicked morsel? I would taste you, my lovely, but I fear I cannot wait any longer.'

'Nor I. Do me now, Josiah.'

Placing a hand on the grass on either side of her, Josiah gave a thrust of his narrow hips and plunged his stout member into Mary's willing body.

Charity felt a potent surge of lust and a warm liquid seeped out of her. She could feel the slippery stuff on the insides of her thighs and wondered if it was normal to seep like that. She soon had evidence that it was. She was unable to take her eyes off Josiah's pumping hips and the dark mouth of Mary's wet quim. When Josiah rose up with each thrust, she could see his balls and the base of his cock and the juicy stem as it slid in and out of the hairy red aperture.

Mary groaned loudly and clutched at Josiah's buttocks. 'Ride me, my lusty,' she moaned. 'Ah, yes. That's the way. Do me. Take me. Cleave me in two. Plough me. Plunder me.'

Urged on by Mary's coarse speech, Josiah's hips wove from side to side as he strove to drive her towards her ultimate pleasure. Mary's plump shapely legs waved in the air. She brought her heels down and dug them into Josiah's buttocks, drubbing at him as if she had been wearing spurs.

'Dear Lord, woman. You hot piece. You're insatiable. You'll be the death of me!' Josiah panted.

'Aye! But what a wonderful way to go!' Mary said. 'More. Give me more. Tup me, my lusty. I am almost at my peak.'

Josiah toiled valiantly, his cock so swollen it looked like a knobbly staff. Bending his head he bit gently at Mary's nipples, then nuzzled her white neck.

'Oh. Oh. I'm spending,' Mary moaned, her face twisting into an expression of the purest pleasure. She lifted her hips, her legs spasming and her heels drumming madly on Josiah's bottom.

'So am I. You have undone me,' Josiah said, his breath expelling in a series of loud grunts. 'Ah God, woman. You've milked me dry.'

Charity pressed her hands into her lap, trying to still the ache and throbbing in her sex, but she knew that nothing would make this new longing go away. Nothing would assuage the hunger inside her, but the touch of a man. Now she truly knew what it was to perform the act of generation. And she understood why the act was bound around with secrecy and rules and prohibitions. For if everyone was to follow his or her own natures, then everyone would be doing 'the act' all the time.

And that would never do, because the sacred and beautiful would become boring and mundane. God's greatest gifts were meant to be treasured.

While Mary and Josiah were lying side by side, stroking each other tenderly in the aftermath of their passion, Charity stole silently away. She felt grateful to Sarah for granting her enlightenment and she felt less angry at the men for making her feel uncomfortable earlier. Now she understood that they were guarding their maleness from the greed of women.

With a secret smile she realised that she now had power over Josiah Wainwright. She did not intend to abuse that power, but surely she ought to be able to dissuade him from running to the minister with tales of her misdeeds.

But her thoughts, as she made her way back to the settlement, did not settle on any of these things. The image which crowded her mind was that of Jacob Hawkins in his shirt-sleeves, the muscles of his forearms flexing as he chopped wood, and the way his taut buttocks rolled maddeningly inside his tight leather breeches.

Already published

BACK IN CHARGE
Mariah Greene

A woman in control. Sexy, successful, sure of herself and of what she wants, Andrea King is an ambitious account handler in a top advertising agency. Life seems sweet, as she heads for promotion and enjoys the attentions of her virile young boyfriend.

But strange things are afoot at the agency. A shake-up is ordered, with the key job of Creative Director in the balance. Andrea has her rivals for the post, but when the chance of winning a major new account presents itself, she will go to any lengths to please her client – and herself . . .

0 7515 1276 1

THE DISCIPLINE OF PEARLS
Susan Swann

A mysterious gift, handed to her by a dark and arrogant stranger. Who was he? How did he know so much about her? How did he know her life was crying out for something different? Something . . . exciting, erotic?

The pearl pendant, and the accompanying card bearing an unknown telephone number, propel Marika into a world of uninhibited sexuality, filled with the promise of a desire she had never thought possible. The Discipline of Pearls . . . an exclusive society that speaks to the very core of her sexual being, bringing with it calls to ecstasies she is powerless to ignore, unwilling to resist . . .

0 7515 1277 X

HOTEL APHRODISIA
Dorothy Starr

The luxury hotel of Bouvier Manor nestles near a spring whose mineral water is reputed to have powerful aphrodisiac qualities. Whether this is true or not, Dani Stratton, the hotel's feisty receptionist, finds concentrating on work rather tricky, particularly when the muscularly attractive Mitch is around.

And even as a mysterious consortium threatens to take over the Manor, staff and guests seem quite unable to control their insatiable thirsts . . .

0 7515 1287 7

AROUSING ANNA
Nina Sheridan

Anna had always assumed she was frigid. At least, that's what her husband Paul had always told her – in between telling her to keep still during their weekly fumblings under the covers and playing the field himself during his many business trips.

But one such trip provides the chance that Anna didn't even know she was yearning for. Agreeing to put up a lecturer who is visiting the university where she works, she expects to be host to a dry, elderly academic, and certainly isn't expecting a dashing young Frenchman who immediately speaks to her innermost desires. And, much to her delight and surprise, the vibrant Dominic proves himself able and willing to apply himself to the task of arousing Anna . . .

0 7515 1222 2

THE WOMEN'S CLUB
Vanessa Davies

Sybarites is a health club with a difference. Its owner, Julia Marquis, has introduced a full range of services to guarantee complete satisfaction. For after their saunas and facials the exclusively female members can enjoy an 'intimate' massage from one of the club's expert masseurs.

And now, with the arrival of Grant Delaney, it seems the privileged clientele of the women's club will be getting even better value for their money. This talented masseur can fulfil any woman's erotic dreams.

Except Julia's . . .

0 7515 1343 1

PLAYING THE GAME
Selina Seymour

Kate has had enough. No longer is she prepared to pander to the whims of lovers who don't love her; no longer will she cater for their desires while neglecting her own.

But in reaching this decision Kate makes a startling discovery: the potency of her sexual urge, now given free rein through her willingness to play men at their own game. And it is an urge that doesn't go unnoticed – whether at her chauvinistic City firm, at the château of a new French client, or in performing the duties of a high-class call girl . . .

0 7515 1189 7

A SLAVE TO HIS KISS
Anastasia Dubois

When her twin sister Cassie goes missing in the South of France, Venetia Fellowes knows she must do everything in her power to find her. But in the dusty village of Valazur, where Cassie was last seen, a strange aura of complicity connects those who knew her, heightened by an atmosphere of unrestrained sexuality.

As her fears for Cassie's safety mount, Venetia turns to the one person who might be able to help: the enigmatic Esteban, a study in sexual mystery whose powerful spell demands the ultimate sacrifice . . .

0 7515 1344 X

SATURNALIA
Zara Devereux

Recently widowed, Heather Logan is concerned about her sex-life. Even when married it was plainly unsatisfactory, and now the prospects for sexual fulfilment look decidedly thin.

After consulting a worldly friend, however, Heather takes his advice and checks in to Tostavyn Grange, a private hotel-cum-therapy centre for sexual inhibition. Heather had been warned about their 'unconventional' methods, but after the preliminary session, in which she is brought to a thunderous climax – her first – she is more than willing to complete the course . . .

0 7515 1342 3

LITTLE, BROWN & CO. ORDER FORM

All X Libris titles are £4.99

Little, Brown and Company, PO Box 50,
Harlow, Essex CM17 0DZ
Tel: 01279 438150   Fax: 01279 439376

Payments can be made as follows: cheque, postal order (payable to Little, Brown and Company) or by credit cards, Visa/Access. Do not send cash or currency. UK customers and B.F.P.O. please allow £1.00 for postage and packing for the first book, plus 50p for the second book, plus 30p for each additional book up to a maximum charge of £3.00 (7 books plus). Overseas customers including Ireland, please allow £2.00 for the first book plus £1.00 for the second book, plus 50p for each additional book.

NAME (Block Letters) ....

....

ADDRESS ....

....

....

☐ I enclose a cheque/postal order made payable to

Little, Brown and Company for £____

☐ I wish to pay by Access/Visa/AMEX* Card

(* delete as appropriate)

Number ☐☐☐☐☐☐☐☐☐☐☐☐☐☐☐☐

Card Expiry Date _____ Signature _____